MW00914864

Crystal is totally i
tor... until she re
can't give.

Crystal's dream vacation didn't include getting kidnapped by
aliens, but then again, her personal abductor is six-plus feet
of irresistible masculinity whose sizzling looks ignite a
blazing hunger inside her.

Unfortunately, the three words that make Crystal shudder... happily-ever-after... seem to be his mantra. He insists
they are soul-mates and his intense desire to please her is
almost unnerving. But she knows that the only one she can
truly depend on is herself. She doesn't plan to settle down
with any man, let alone one from another world.

Terrien is prepared to woo his *tanash'ae* gently, despite
the hunger blazing through him, but the first time they're
alone, she eagerly throws herself into his arms. Unfortunately, his elation at their passionate encounter is short lived
when she makes it clear she doesn't believe in true love.

Undaunted, he is determined to convince her that they
are meant to be together, no matter what it takes.

Rebel Mate is the third book in Opal Carew's exciting sci-fi
romance series, Abducted. If you enjoy an intense, sexy love story
with an adventurous take-charge woman and the man determined
to prove to her that giving in to love doesn't mean giving up her
freedom, then you'll love this book!

∿

Abducted Series

(sci-fi alien abduction erotic romance novellas)

Forbidden Mate
Unwilling Mate
Rebel Mate
Illicit Mate
Captive Mate

Thanks to all my wonderful Patrons!

Print - Premium

Tiffany Tyson

Print - New Releases

Patricia Klasen

Ebook - New Releases

Jodi Schmedje
Lori Olmstead Cipot

Alcee Clayborne
Beverlee A. Browning
Cheryl Byers
Darlene Good
Doug Williamson
Hilary Beckford
Jamie Graves
Jane Barlow
Jane Davis
Julia Murdock
Kathy Sanford
Lisa Diamond
Lori Hoffman
Maragaret Noble
Sarah Kiefer
Sharon Manning-Lew
Teresa-Lynne Zelych
Vanessa A. Pugh

Victoria Troemel
William L. Suttles

Hot Stuff!

Mandy Rosko

Becky Nelson

REBEL MATE

ABDUCTED SERIES - BOOK 3

OPAL CAREW

To
Marissa,
Queen of the North

CHAPTER 1

"I wonder if those two come as a pair." Crystal smiled at the two gorgeous men sitting at the next table, glancing her way. "I'd definitely be up for that."

Kate, the young woman next to Crystal at the round table, giggled. Next to Kate sat Jenna, who also laughed, a slight blush coloring her cheeks. Across from Crystal, Eva, the fourth woman, smiled.

These woman she was sitting with, all of them strangers, were quite different from one another. Jenna's lovely wide eyes watched everything with avid curiosity and she seemed fascinated by Crystal. Crystal was used to that from other women, but most had a disapproving air toward her relaxed attitude about sex. She sensed none of that from Jenna. Nor from Kate, for that matter. Kate, a few years younger than the rest of them, seemed to have an adventurous spirit but still lacked experience and confidence.

Eva seemed more reserved. Just her classic little black dress and pearls said volumes about her. Yet Crystal felt a connection to this woman. If they lived in the same city, rather than having met at a holiday resort, Crystal wondered if they might be friends. Most people would think one couldn't tell that much about someone after knowing them for only an hour or so in such a casual setting, but Crystal had a good instinct about people. She could tell that Eva might come off as tight-assed to most people, but Crystal was sure it was because she had learned to be cautious. Probably because she'd been hurt by some man. In fact, she was probably recently divorced, judging by how she often ran her thumb over her ring finger where a wedding band would sit.

That wouldn't happen to Crystal. She didn't intend to get married. And she sure as hell wouldn't be hurt by a guy. She'd never get emotionally involved enough for that to happen. Not that she had anything against marriage. It would just tie her down too damn much. She loved sex way too much for that. And variety. One man would just never do.

She glanced around the large ballroom at the plethora of exquisitely gorgeous, fuckable men. This was some sensational welcome party. And this resort was five-star all the way. She worked in the marketing department of a chain of luxury hotels and this place rivaled her chain in every way.

She had to admit, it was nice to be a guest for a change. This next week, she intended to relax on the beach, swim, read some steamy books…and meet men. She was in dire need of sexual distraction. For the past couple of weeks, her libido had been in overdrive. She was always ready for a good fuck with a willing and able man, but lately, her yearning had intensified a hundredfold. And when she tried to satisfy that longing with a good long fuck session, it barely took the edge off.

God damn it, but she was starting to think she'd go insane if she didn't find something to meet the intense need gnawing at her insides. Her gaze caught on an exceptionally good-looking man two tables over, who filled out his tuxedo jacket quite nicely with broad shoulders and thick muscular arms. Her gaze fell to his trousers, but she couldn't get a feel for what he was packing. He definitely had potential, though. Her gaze shifted to his face and his brilliant smile…then she realized he was smiling at a woman approaching the table. Crystal's glance shifted to his ring finger and—damn it—there was a gold band. Fuck, she was slipping.

Crystal took a sip of the sweet red cocktail in front of her, the specialty for this evening. Eva's gaze was turned to the left and Crystal noticed the hostess leading another woman, holding one of the red cocktails in her hand, to their table. In a black tailored suit and with her golden-blonde hair swept back from her face in a neat up-do, she looked like she'd just left the office. The woman tugged at the hem of her trim jacket, glancing around uncertainly. She definitely needed to learn to relax.

"This is where you'll be sitting this evening," the hostess said over the music and laughter as they approached the table. "Please help yourself to drinks and appetizers. Someone will come and get you for the orientation in about twenty minutes."

The blonde nodded her thanks and settled in the empty chair. Eva smiled at her.

"Hi. My name's Eva."

Eva offered her hand and the other woman shook it.

"Hi. I'm Aria."

Eva's fingers glided along the simple string of pearls she wore at her neck. The pearls paired with the flattering black wraparound dress gave her an air of elegance and femininity, a sharp contrast to the professional, business tone of Aria's power suit.

"This is Jenna, Kate and Crystal." Eva introduced the women clockwise around the table.

They all smiled and nodded. All but Aria wore an evening gown.

"I feel a little out of place." Aria fiddled with the clip holding her hair in a twist at the back of her head. "I should have worn something else."

"Don't worry about it," Eva said. "You look great."

"Thanks."

Crystal admired the way Eva put the woman at ease. She seemed the quintessential hostess. Or maybe it was more a need to nurture. It was something Crystal wished she could do herself, but she didn't really know how to connect with other women.

"This is so exciting!" Kate pushed her long, auburn hair behind her ear, her green eyes glittering with enthusiasm. "I wonder what they have planned for us."

Aria sipped the drink she still held in her hand.

"I don't know, but I hope there are men involved." Crystal openly admired the hard, muscular butts of three gorgeous guys in their early twenties as they passed by. She watched them as they approached a table with several other young men. Maybe later she'd strike up a conversation with them and see where things might lead. Maybe one or two or even three hard young bodies might satisfy the craving deep inside her.

"There certainly are a lot of good-looking men here," said Kate.

"And women," Jenna said.

Crystal glanced in the same direction as Jenna to see a pair of blonde women in low-cut gowns pass by, their generous, round breasts practically bouncing out of their dresses. The women had all the obvious attractions that made a man drool, but Jenna had them beat. Jenna's short feathery black hair framed her wide blue eyes, high cheekbones and sweet smile. She had a flawless complexion and a lovely figure, too. Yet she seemed uncertain of her own allure.

"Don't worry about those two, honey. They've got lots

out here…" Crystal indicated her chest, then waved her hand by her head. "But not much up here. Not like you." She laid her hand on Jenna's. "You've got brains and looks. In fact, you're way better looking than most of the women here."

When Crystal had arrived at the table, Jenna and Eva had been talking about the fact that Jenna taught English at a college. Brains and good looks. What more could a woman want?

Jenna smiled at Crystal, but as soon as Crystal drew her hand away, Jenna tucked hers under the table. Crystal sensed uneasiness in the other woman and she had a feeling it wasn't just from being touched by a stranger. With the slight flush of her cheeks and the way she avoided looking in Crystal's direction, Crystal wondered if maybe Jenna was a little confused…sexually speaking.

Not that Crystal minded a little girl-on-girl action every now and again. She sensed Jenna had never tried being with another woman. Maybe after Crystal had satisfied her intense craving for cock, she'd suggest Jenna join her and some hunk in a threesome, just to help Jenna explore her curiosity. Crystal would have to work at loosening her up a bit along the way. Opening her mind to the possibilities of sexual activities other than boy meets girl, boy fucks girl. So many women seemed so stuck in a rut.

The thought of cocks and fucking sent heat thrumming through her. She locked gazes with a gorgeous man two tables over. He glanced her way and she sent him a seductive smile. His dark eyes glittered and he smiled back. Hmm. A definite possibility.

But she wanted to spend a little more time getting to know these women first. It would be nice to have friends to spend the days sunning and laughing with.

"With all these sexy hunks to choose from," Crystal said,

"I plan to get laid every night by a different man." She winked at Eva. "Or two."

Kate grinned and Jenna turned her gaze to her glossy sapphire blue polished nails that matched her dress.

A waitress stopped beside the table. "More drinks, ladies?"

Eva nodded. The waitress took away the empty glasses and set down five new ones. Eva picked one up and sipped.

The man Crystal had been making eyes at stood up and started walking toward the table.

CHAPTER 2

"And here comes contestant number one," Crystal purred.

He smiled and leaned close to Crystal. "You are incredibly sexy and I'd love to dance with you. Shall we start vertically?"

She chuckled at the corny line. He was hot and sexy, despite his lack of imagination. When it came to sex, she had enough imagination for the both of them.

He took her hand and led her to the dance floor where he drew her close to his hard chest. It was what she'd been craving—being pressed close to a solid masculine body, the prospect of sex imminent—but for some reason, the thought of being with this man did not lessen the craving for…something. What that something was, she couldn't tell, but it gnawed at her insides. She didn't understand it. This man was extremely do-able.

As she danced, she tried to relax into it, to let out the party girl in her, but this just didn't seem right. Whatever that meant. She just couldn't get into this guy. And if she wasn't into him, he wasn't getting into her.

The song changed and Crystal drew away. "Thanks."

He grinned. "So my place or yours?"

"Ah, no, I mean I'm going back to join my friends."

She began walking off the dance floor.

He frowned. "You're kidding, right? After sending me those 'come fuck me' looks, you're just walking away?"

She simply shrugged as she continued strolling away. It must be her jerk-meter that had kicked in. That was why this guy wasn't working for her. She returned to the table and wrapped her hands around her glass.

The women glanced at her expectantly.

"He was nice," Crystal said, "but not exactly what I'm looking for."

"And what are you looking for?" Kate asked.

"I don't know, but I'm sure I'll know it when I find it." At least, she hoped she would.

Crystal stabbed the cherry in her glass with the sharp end of the swizzle stick and brought it to her lips. She gently tugged it off with her teeth, then drew it into her mouth, closing her lips around it.

Jenna watched with fascination, then nervously glanced down at her hands.

"You know, I won this vacation in a contest." Jenna twirled the tip of her finger around the rim of her glass

"Really? I did too," Eva responded.

Kate's eyes widened. "Me too."

Crystal glanced around, then pointed at Aria. "And you?"

Aria nodded.

"Same here." Crystal sipped her drink.

"Omigod." Kate giggled. "What a coincidence."

"Not a coincidence, sweetie. They probably want to get a photo of all of us. You know, for marketing, yada yada yada." Crystal rested her chin on her hands. "And we'll probably have to sit through some long, boring pitch to buy a timeshare."

"I don't think so," Aria chimed in. "We're not exactly the demographic they're looking for and—"

"Ladies, my name is Baryn. It's time for the orientation."

Crystal glanced up to see a man standing beside the table.

Good God, he was gorgeous. Tall with broad shoulders and muscles bulging under his well-tailored jacket. He smiled at them with dazzling white teeth and she was ready to drop her panties right here and now.

"Would you all come with me, please?"

He drew back Kate's chair and offered his hand.

Kate sent him a glowing smile as she took it and stood up. "Lead on."

Crystal leaned toward Aria and murmured, "I would absolutely *come* with him. Anywhere. Anytime."

Aria giggled. Crystal and the others stood and Baryn led them across the ballroom, his hand resting on the small of Kate's back.

Eva seemed to have trouble keeping her gaze from locking on the man's rock-hard butt as he walked away from the table. And Crystal couldn't blame her. Crystal, on the other hand, didn't resist the urge.

When they stepped into the atrium, a prickle started at the back of Crystal's neck, then skated down her spine as heat washed through her. She turned to see a devastatingly handsome man watching them. His dark glittering eyes fixed on her, so intense she thought they'd burn through her.

Now *that* was definitely what she was looking for.

At over six feet tall, with the same muscular physique as Baryn, he was a magnificent specimen of manhood. He had full sexy lips she could imagine moving across her skin, a square jaw she'd love to stroke, and thick, wavy, sable brown hair shimmering with bronze highlights that she longed to glide her fingers through.

She'd told Aria she would come anywhere, anytime with

Baryn, but the way her libido was spinning out of control with this new guy, if she were merely to brush against him, *anywhere anytime* might just be *right here right now*.

"This is my associate, Terrien," Baryn said.

"Good evening, ladies," Terrien said with a beaming smile.

Though he spoke to all of them, his glowing green gaze settled on her. Her breath locked in her lungs as a need more intense than anything she'd ever experienced before surged through her.

If there were any way on Earth to make it happen—and she was sure she'd find one—she'd be stroking his muscular butt within the next couple of hours, as she devoured what she prayed was his spectacularly huge cock.

"This way." He gestured toward a corridor on the left.

"Aren't the elevators the other way?" Jenna asked.

"The normal ones, yes," Terrien answered, "but we're taking the VIP elevator."

"Mmm, VIP. That's my kind of action," Crystal murmured to Aria and Jenna.

Kate walked beside Baryn, Eva walked a couple feet behind them, and Crystal followed with Jenna and Aria. Terrien fell in behind as Baryn led them down a narrow corridor, then opened a door labeled "Authorized Personnel Only". At the end of another narrow corridor, they came to an elevator. Terrien pushed a key into a lock on the control panel, and the doors opened. They crowded into the small space, and the doors closed.

"This doesn't look very VIP to me," Crystal grumbled, gazing around at the small, ordinary-looking elevator.

Her attention immediately switched back to Terrien. Standing in such close proximity to the man sent her temperature rising, even though he had chosen to stand on the other side of the elevator with four women between them. Still, his gaze kept flickering in her direction. Her whole body tensed and the deep yearning that had been building for weeks flashed hotter.

God, she wanted this man. And she didn't know why. Well, she knew why. She was horny and he was extremely sexy. But she'd never wanted a man so desperately. The intensity of it unnerved her.

If the other women hadn't been in the confined space with them, she would have stopped the elevator and torn off his clothes immediately. Her heartbeat accelerated and the world started spinning out of control. Then she realized the elevator seemed to have sped up. It jostled a little from side to side. Aria swayed sideways and grabbed on to Crystal's arm. Crystal placed her hand over Aria's and glanced at the other woman. Aria had gone as white as a sheet and she looked as though she might throw up.

"You okay, honey?" Crystal asked. "You look a little green."

Eva clasped Aria's other hand. "You don't look well."

"I'm sure she'll be fine in a minute," Baryn said.

The doors opened, and Kate, Baryn and Jenna stepped out. Aria took a step or two and then her knees started to buckle. Crystal grabbed one of Aria's arms and Eva took the other. They steadied her as they helped her from the elevator.

They entered a moderate-size room with upholstered armchairs facing one wall. The décor had changed dramatically from the coral and green they'd seen everywhere else in the hotel. Also missing were the warm wooden details. This room was cool blue with very minimalist, clean lines.

Crystal paused, feeling a little dizzy herself, whether from the disorienting elevator ride, the jarring change in environment, or the sudden distance from Terrien, she didn't know.

Eva led Aria to a chair.

"I don't know what came over me." Aria's cheeks flushed red.

"The transporter has that effect on some people."

Crystal turned toward the unfamiliar female voice.

"The what?" Aria's eyes widened.

A striking woman with a cool expression and an authoritative air stood beside Baryn, who was taking off his suit jacket. The woman handed him a dark green jacket just like the one she wore and he pulled it on. It looked like a military uniform of some sort.

Crystal's gaze shifted to Terrien, who had already donned a similar jacket and her heart fluttered. She stared mesmerized at his broad chest and muscular arms.

Oh, God, she loved a man in uniform.

"The transporter," the newcomer repeated.

The woman's long, straight hair was pulled back tight from her face and fastened into a ponytail on top of her head. It was so light it was almost white, but it shimmered with soft lavender highlights when she moved. She pushed a button on a small console on the wall beside her, triggering a loud humming.

The wall started to slide upward, revealing windows beyond. Aria gasped, echoed by several of the others, as a stunning vista of stars was revealed.

"It transported you to our starship."

"That's ridiculous." Crystal wondered if this was some kind of space fantasy camp or something, but she wasn't interested. She wanted a man, a bed, and a solid cock. And the bed was optional. All this space-fantasy crap would just get in the way of her getting laid.

She stepped to the window and peered outside. Still, they'd done a great job on the display behind the glass. She could almost swear she was looking out at a real star field.

"I don't know, Crystal." Kate's voice sounded on the edge of panic. "Look!" She pointed upward.

Crystal followed her gaze. The wall panels continued to retreat over the ceiling, revealing a beautiful but quite disturbing view of Earth.

"Oh, my God." Eva sank into a chair, sounding a little panicked. "We've just been abducted by aliens."

CHAPTER 3

Crystal stared at the big blue planet, her heart pounding. Could this really be happening?

She glanced around at the other women's faces. All of them were in a state of shock. She turned back to the window, but her gaze caught on Terrien.

He was watching her.

Her heart pounded faster as their gazes locked. His eyes, a striking forest green, were filled with a concerned, almost protective, glow.

Her chest tightened, unnerved at being the center of his attention.

At the same time, she wanted him to have eyes only for her. She wanted to believe that he was staring at her because he wanted her so badly he could barely stop himself from dragging her into his arms and backing her up against the wall, then—

Oh, God. She sucked in a breath before her wicked daydream went too far. She had to keep her wits about her.

"You."

Crystal's gaze darted to the uniformed woman who now pointed at Aria.

"Come with me."

Crystal didn't like the sound of that.

"We stay together," Eva insisted as she stood up and walked toward Aria protectively.

"No, actually you don't," the woman responded in a commanding tone.

As Aria stood up on shaky legs, Crystal stepped forward too but stopped in her tracks when Terrien moved in front of Eva. He wasn't menacing, but Eva seemed reluctant to push past him. Did he have the same effect on Eva as he did on her, or was it simply that he was tall, strong and masculine?

Oh, God, intensely masculine. She could imagine his strong hand grasping her arm, the heat of his body close to hers as he restrained her. Then the feel of his lips against hers as he took her mouth with a wild passion.

She sucked in a deep breath as she pulled herself back to the here and now. Something very strange was going on around them and all she could think about was one of the hot hunks responsible for kidnapping them.

She licked her lips as she watched the uniformed woman lead Aria to a door, which slid open as they approached. A couple more uniformed men appeared and herded Crystal and the others toward another door. They were jostled together as they were urged into a corridor, led past several doors, then around a corner to the right. A moment later, they found themselves in another room, this one smaller than the last, with a couple of easy chairs and a couch around a large, oval coffee table. Terrien didn't follow them into the room and Crystal felt an immediate sense of loss.

Crystal and the others sat on the couch and huddled

together. Crystal's heart thundered in her chest. Something very strange was going on, but alien abduction?

"Where's Kate?" Jenna asked, her voice thin.

Crystal's body tensed as she glanced around and realized Kate was nowhere to be seen.

Eva patted Jenna's hand. "It's okay. Everything will be all right."

Eva spoke in a calm tone, but Crystal could tell that was just a façade. She was certain Eva felt as freaked out as Crystal did right now.

But Crystal refused to be a meek little lamb cowering in a corner. She glared at the two uniformed men standing between them and the door.

"What is going on?" she demanded.

As if on cue, the door slid open. Crystal turned to see another gorgeous hunk of man step into the room. His honey-blond hair fell in waves to his shoulders and his uniform jacket, adorned with three small gold ovals on the stand-up collar, hugged his broad, muscled chest.

The man's deep turquoise eyes turned to Eva and her breathing seemed to stop. He smiled, and Eva's breath expelled. Crystal watched as Eva's wide-eyed gaze remained locked on him as he moved to stand in front of them. This man seemed to be having the same effect on Eva as Terrien had on Crystal.

"Good evening, ladies. I'd like to welcome you to our ship, the *Patira Alana*. I am Commander Larson Raa-ling, the first officer. I'm sure this has been quite a shock for you."

"Yeah, no kidding," Crystal said.

"I want to assure you, you will not be harmed," he continued.

"What do you want from us?" Jenna asked, her voice quavering.

"Let me explain why we have brought you here."

He sat in the chair facing them and settled back into the cushioned upholstery. The tapered line of his uniform accentuated his broad shoulders and slim waist. From the fascinated expression on Eva's face, she seemed to be mentally stripping away his uniform piece by piece.

Crystal could imagine his dark green jacket slipping away, followed by the shirt beneath, to reveal muscular arms and tight, ridged stomach muscles. He was a fine specimen and she would love to fuck him, but when she tried to imagine it, images of Terrien replaced him.

"There is a power in the universe that takes a hand in our lives," the commander said. "We call it *nata'tai*. It provides the means to keep us healthy, as individuals and as races."

"We don't want a lesson in alien religion," Crystal sniped.

"To stay healthy," he continued, "a race must grow. It must embrace other cultures. It must open its gene pool to other races, otherwise it will stagnate. Physically, emotionally and culturally."

"Oh, my God, they've brought us here as breeding stock." Jenna's face paled.

Breeding stock? Crystal glanced at the other two women.

Eva held Jenna's hand, her lips a tight line. Crystal sensed she was nearing the end of her rope. Eva stared at Commander Raa-ling and shifted in her seat. Her face went pale and she seemed absolutely terrified.

"You have not been brought here to be sex slaves," the commander reassured. "As a race matures, *nata'tai* gives its people the ability to sense their *tanash'ae*—what you would call their soul-mate—even over great distances. To ensure a mingling of races, *nata'tai* directs the spirits of *tanash'aei*—soul-mates—to be born in different races on different planets."

"Soul-mates?" Jenna repeated in a hushed tone.

"That's right. Each of you is the soul-mate of a member of

this crew. *That's* why you've been brought here. To meet your *tanash'ae.*"

"So you intend to convince us we're in love with some guy, *then* use us for breeding," Crystal scoffed.

"This has nothing to do with procreation. I'm talking about love." He focused directly on Eva. "The love of two people destined to be together. Of people who make each other complete. Soul-mates. *Tanish'aei.*"

Eva seemed mesmerized by his words.

"Excuse me, Commander." The woman who'd dragged Aria away stood in the doorway. She had two gold ovals on her collar, while the two men who stood by the door had none. Possibly they were a symbol of rank.

"Captain wants to see senior staff."

"Thank you, Casey." The commander rose. "Excuse me, ladies. You will remain here until someone is free to take you to your quarters. Make yourselves comfortable."

He followed Casey, the female officer, out of the room, followed by the other two men. The door slid closed behind them, leaving Crystal, Eva and Jenna alone in the room.

Crystal rose and approached the door, but it didn't open. She flattened her hand on it, then dragged her fingers along the edge, searching for a way to trigger the mechanism.

"Are you okay, Eva?" Jenna asked, sliding her arm around Eva's shoulders.

"Did you feel…funny…when that man came into the room?" Eva asked.

"What do you mean?" Jenna asked.

"She means were we hot for him." Crystal turned to face them.

Eva shot her a glance and Crystal shrugged.

"You were practically drooling over him, sweetie." Crystal crossed the room and sat beside Eva. "He is definitely a hunk, but I find that other one—Terrien, I think they called him—much hotter. I really would love to jump his bones."

That was the understatement of the century.

"Crystal, how can you think about that now?" Jenna asked. "We've been kidnapped by people from another planet."

"That's the key. They are people. Just like us."

Eva shook her head. "How can you treat this so lightly?"

"We're here," Crystal responded. "I figure I'll make the best of it. At home, a lay is a lay, but here..." She shrugged. "Well, who knows what special talents these alien hunks have?"

"They said they know who our soul-mates are." Jenna stared into space.

"That might be what they believe, but I don't buy it." Crystal didn't believe in soul-mates.

"Me neither," Eva agreed.

After about twenty minutes, the door slid open, and Commander Raa-ling entered, followed by Casey and Terrien. Crystal's body tingled with awareness of Terrien's masculine presence.

"You'll be taken to your quarters now," Commander Raa-ling said to all of them. "If you have any more questions, pose them to your *tanash'ae*."

Casey approached Jenna and Terrien stepped toward Crystal. She stood up, feeling almost panicky at the increasing strength of his effect on her as he moved closer. He gazed into her eyes, then smiled and the breath locked in her lungs. Oh, God, she needed to have this man. She desperately needed him to satisfy the intense craving deep inside her. He turned and she followed him toward the door.

Eva leapt to her feet and stepped in front of them. "Don't go with them. If we stay together, we have a better chance."

"A better chance to what, Eva?" Crystal asked. She leaned close to Eva's ear and murmured, "Look, I don't believe in soul-mates, but I'm damned curious about sex with an alien. Especially one that looks like this hunk." She glanced toward Terrien, then back to Eva and winked, then followed him toward the door.

"It's time to go," Casey insisted.

Eva grasped Jenna's sleeve.

"Don't go," Eva implored.

Eva's gaze locked on Jenna's.

"I'm sorry, Eva." Jenna's large, blue eyes pleaded for understanding.

CHAPTER 4

Crystal felt a little guilty abandoning Eva, but she could not ignore the need driving her forward. Eva would be fine with the handsome Commander Raa-ling, Crystal was sure. Clearly, Eva felt an attraction to him similar to what Crystal felt with Terrien, but Eva was fighting it. If it was anywhere near as strong as what Crystal felt for Terrien, Eva would get past her resistance soon enough.

Jenna and her guard followed Crystal and Terrien out of the room and the door slid closed behind them.

Crystal followed Terrien down the corridor and around some turns, watching his fine, tight butt as he walked. Finally, he stopped in front of a door and it slid open, then she followed him into what appeared to be a private quarters. The décor was simple but comfortable, with dark wood furniture, probably simulated but looking quite authentic, and upholstered chairs and couch with clean but inviting lines.

Terrien took off his uniform jacket and hung it on a hook as Crystal glanced around. He kept his distance, just watching her.

"Mmm. Nice place."

"I'll show you your room."

She followed him through another door into a room with a large bed, then to another door and yet another bedroom. It was roomy and looked very comfortable.

"This is where I'll be sleeping?" she asked.

"That's right."

She gazed at him and his smoldering forest green eyes bored into her, ratcheting up the heat simmering through her body. God, she wanted this man in bed right now, but sleeping was *not* what she had in mind. She turned and, with a seductive sway to her hips, sauntered into the bigger bedroom. She stood beside the bed and stroked the velvety navy bedcovers.

"I like it in here. Whose room is this?"

"Mine."

The moment Terrien had seen Crystal in the ballroom, his heart had accelerated, his blood heating, his need for her surging to a new level of desperation. This woman was his *tanash'ea*. The woman he would spend his life with. He was deeply in love with her.

He longed to touch her honey-blonde hair. To coil his fingers through it. To breath in the scent of it. He wanted to capture her soft, ruby lips, to feel her heart beating against his.

The glittering red dress she wore hugged her body like a second skin, showing every delightful curve. He had to fight the urge to grab her and drag her into his arms. To tear off her clothes and drive into her until they both screamed in ecstasy. His cock was in a constant state of readiness. It had been sheer torture meeting with the Earth women and bringing them aboard while trying to ignore his need to sweep Crystal into his arms and possess her.

Now he stood alone in his bedroom with her. Private. Intimate. His hormones spiking through him. He could just reach for her and...

He sucked in a breath, knowing he had to keep a careful check on his rising desire. He had to be sensitive to her needs. Wait until she was ready.

She smiled seductively and strolled toward him. She ran her hands along his shoulders and he gritted his teeth as her touch jolted his need toward the breaking point.

"Are you my match?" she asked.

"Yes, I am your *tanash'ae*." He tried to keep his voice even, but it came out a little hoarse.

She stroked her hand down his chest, her lovely blue eyes glittering. He clamped his hand over hers, stilling it.

"Ever since I first sensed your presence, I have hungered for you. As we got closer to your world, the hunger became a desperate craving. Do not toy with me, if you don't intend to follow through. I may not be able to hold myself back."

"Honey, I don't want you to hold back."

He stood frozen. Had he heard her correctly? Was it possible he didn't understand the nuance of her language well enough, because surely she couldn't be as willing as she seemed. He'd studied Earth and her culture and he and his shipmates understood that it would take some time and patience before these women, with their different sexual mores, would be ready to consummate their soul-mate relationship.

He tensed as she released his top button. She leaned forward and her lips grazed the base of his neck. His head began to spin as her fingers stroked down his chest, then released the next button. A shudder of pure, unadulterated lust coursed through him.

Gattra, he couldn't handle much more of this.

His hands closed around her shoulders, her soft skin tempting him beyond reason. She slid her hand down to his waist, then released the top button of his pants.

His carefully maintained restraint abandoned him in a flash and he grabbed the sides of her evening gown and tore it open. His gaze fell on her as she stood before him in a red lace bra that only covered the bottoms of her breasts, leaving her nipples totally exposed. Round, pebbled areolas with rigid nipples standing hard and ready.

"*Gattra*," he exclaimed.

Now we're getting somewhere. Crystal smiled, watching his green eyes turn a deep moss as his gaze swept over her.

She grabbed his shirt and tore it open, then stared at his impressively broad chest. Her gaze wandered back to his face, with his full, sexy lips and glimmering dark green eyes. God, what a sexy man. Especially the way he gazed at her, as if she were the sexiest woman alive.

Longing to feel his body against hers, she stepped forward and pressed herself to his chest, sighing at the delicious sensation of his hard muscled flesh against her pebbling nipples. She nibbled his collarbone. He cupped her breast and his fingers found her rigid nipple. His scorching touch took her breath away. He cupped her cheek with his free hand and lifted her face, then captured her lips. His tongue plunged into her mouth and she felt faint at the searing intensity. Her tongue tangled around his and she sucked it, unable to get enough of him.

Oh, God, she needed him. Her insides ached with desperate longing. He released her lips and she glided down his chin, then nuzzled his neck. Her hands fumbled for his zipper and she dragged it down and unfastened the button.

"Mmm. Baby," she murmured in his ear. "Let me see what you've got for me."

She almost gasped as her fingers found the hard, hot flesh stretched over an impressively thick shaft. She drew it from the fabric and stared with wide eyes. God, it was impressive. It had to be ten inches long and she could barely get her fingers around it.

She licked her lips, then knelt in front of him.

Terrien's insides clenched as she lowered to her knees, the look of awe on her face inflating his male ego as much as his desire for her inflated his erection. When her lips touched his corona, he groaned. He had to stop himself from surging forward to impale her mouth with his aching cock.

The tip of her tongue lapped over him and nudged against the small opening, then she opened wide and his cockhead slid into her warm, moist mouth. He sucked in a breath at the exquisite sensation. She swirled her tongue over him, then sucked gently. Heat blasted through him. Her hands wrapped around him and she stroked.

Gattra, he couldn't stand it. He grasped her shoulders and pulled her to her feet, then merged his lips with hers. He drove his tongue into her like he wanted to do with his cock. Deep into her hot moistness. He cupped her soft, round breast, reveling in the feel of her silky skin and the hard nipple spearing into his palm. Her warm hand glided up and down his shaft, escalating his need.

Dahran, he had to have her.

But he didn't want to rush her.

She drew back and smiled broadly, her blue eyes glittering with need. Seeing her body, practically naked in the tiny bra, skimpy panties and garter belt, made him swell more. Her hand tightened around his erection and she pumped enthusiastically.

"I want you inside me right now," Crystal murmured.

He groaned, barely able to hold back. Slowly and steadily, he backed her to the wall and kissed her again, swirling his tongue inside her mouth. She leaned back and opened her legs, then guided his cock along the smooth skin of her taut stomach and across the silk of her panties. Somehow the fabric of the crotch parted and...

Gattra. He felt her wet opening against his aching cockhead and he buried his face in her hair, groaning softly. Reeling in his intense desire to impale her with one deep thrust, he eased forward slowly, allowing his cockhead to push into her softness just a little. His head spun at the intensity of wild sensations bursting through him.

"Oh, shove it in, baby," she murmured against his ear. "I want to feel that beautiful hard cock of yours driving into me."

He almost lost it at her words, but somehow he clung to his resolve and eased forward only a little more into the heavenly warmth of her body.

She wrapped her hands around his buttocks and tried to pull him into her, but with a strength of will he didn't know he possessed, he continued easing into her slowly, filling her a little at a time, her moist flesh stretching around his hard, aching cock.

She sucked in a breath as he filled her deeper and deeper. Her lips played along the side of his neck and the soft sounds she murmured encouraged him.

CHAPTER 5

Crystal couldn't believe how big and hard he was inside her, stretching her delightfully. He continued to fill her, on and on, until finally he was fully immersed. He leaned against her, crushing her to the wall.

Feeling trapped by his strong, masculine body thrilled her. Her breasts swelled with need. Her breathing, slow and heavy, barely sustained her.

Terrien drew in a deep breath, then tipped up her chin and claimed her lips in a potently erotic kiss, his tongue thoroughly exploring the inside of her mouth. When he released her, she gasped for air. His gaze locked on to hers, holding her mesmerized as he drew back, the head of his penis dragging along the length of her vagina, stimulating her with exquisite pleasure. Then he slid forward, impaling her again.

She wrapped her arms around his shoulders, dragging in deep breaths as he drew back and glided forward several more times. Her body rigid with need, she pivoted forward and back with his movements.

Pleasure swelled through her in waves. He spiraled his

hips against hers, sending her head spinning. As his sure hands cupped her buttocks and lifted her, she wrapped her legs around him and arched forward, gasping as his cock pushed even deeper inside her.

Oh, God, yes, she was going to come soon. Her body stiffened and she tightened around him, almost gasping at the feel of his thick cock cradled inside her.

"Relax, sweetheart," he murmured in her ear.

But she couldn't relax. She wanted an orgasm so badly it hurt, and she knew she had to work for it. She squeezed her internal muscles and pulled on him, sucking him deep into her body. She wanted this orgasm. She would not let it slip away.

"Fuck me. Oh, God, fuck me hard."

His moss-green eyes seared her with his intense desire. He began to move, driving that big cock of his deep inside her. Again and again. Heavenly sensations quivered through her.

She slid her fingers between them, finding her clitoris. As he plunged into her, she rubbed rapidly at her clit, stimulating, feeling the intensity build. He tried to draw her hand away, but she resisted, pulsing against herself as he pumped into her.

"You don't need to do that," he murmured against her ear, then kissed the base of her neck.

"Yes, I do." Her guttural voice sounded so needy, she barely recognized it. "God, please just fuck me. I'm so close."

He relented and thrust deep into her, pounding her against the wall. The sensation of his rigid cock thrusting inside her and her fingers stimulating herself brought the elusive orgasm close. He thrust deep again, pinning her to the wall, nearly melting her to a puddle of mush. Then he stormed her mouth with his tongue, thrusting deep into her just as he had with his cock. Her insides ached with yearning and she wanted to beg him to continue fucking her, but his mouth on hers, his tongue driving into her, nearly sent her over the edge.

Then he began to move again. His cock drove in deep and hard.

"Oh, my God, I'm coming." Totally shocked, she found herself flying over the edge.

She clung to him tightly, their bodies crushed together, his cock filling her impossibly full, and she rode the wave of ecstasy. Never had an orgasm come so easily.

He thrust sharply and she felt him erupt inside her. Her whole being shimmered with intense explosions of blissful joy.

Finally, she slumped against him and his arms tightened around her. He lowered her legs, but remained buried inside her.

"That was…wonderful."

He kissed her neck. "It would be even more wonderful if you relaxed and let me pleasure you."

Oh, damn, she'd bruised his male ego.

"Honey, you did." She nuzzled his neck, then beamed at him. "You were incredible."

She kissed his cheek lightly and intended to ease out of his embrace, but he held her still. He gazed into her eyes and stroked her cheek.

"Crystal, you don't have to stimulate yourself. I know how to bring you to orgasm without that."

She stroked his jaw. Male ego was one thing, but he needed to understand. Although she loved being fucked by a man, ultimately she took responsibility for her own pleasure. She would not depend on a man for that.

"Look, sweetie, don't worry about it. It's just that I know my body better than you do."

"Give me a chance to prove it."

His cock twitched inside her. He drew it out, then swept her into his arms and carried her to the bed. He laid her down and stretched out beside her, then unfastened her bra and peeled it away, smiling appreciatively as he released her thirty-eight D breasts. His mouth covered her rigid nipple and he licked the beadlike nub, washing her in pleasure. He kissed down her belly and as he approached her crotchless panties, she opened her legs, knowing she revealed the thin strip of silky blonde curls and the pink folds of flesh between them.

"*Gattra*, my love. This garment is quite…*fasvin*."

She didn't know what it meant, but from the awe in his voice, it sounded wicked and wonderful.

His tongue nudged against her pussy, then dabbed at her clit. She was still so primed, she nearly climaxed right then and there.

Two more licks and another nudge and the pleasure swamped her senses. She arched against him.

"Oh, God, you're making me come *again*." She couldn't believe it. Blissful sensations blazed through her and she catapulted over the edge.

Never had she had two orgasms so close together.

He continued to lick, driving her on and on, her moan intensifying with the pleasure pulsing through her, until finally she collapsed on the bed.

He smiled and prowled up beside her, then took her in his arms and kissed her sweetly. The blissful feel of being in his tender embrace disturbed her. She had to break the intimate contact.

She reached for his rock-hard cock and stroked it, surprised that it was still rigid with wanting her.

"It's your turn now, honey."

She pushed herself up and crouched over him, then grasped his incredible cock in her hands and licked the head.

It twitched under her attention. She swirled her tongue around him, then licked him top to bottom.

Her hands slid around his shaft and she pumped him as she swallowed the head into her mouth. She took him deep, then squeezed her lips as she drew back. Keeping his cockhead in her mouth, she swirled her tongue under the corona, around and around the ridge.

"Crystal, sweetheart, you're going to make me—ah."

She drew back with a smile, stroking his stiff cock with her hands.

"That's the idea, honey. I want you to... ahhh."

"I am trying to hold myself back."

"You seem to make a habit of that." She swirled her tongue over his cockhead again, then smiled at him. "Come on, show me how much you love my mouth sucking your big cock. Shoot a load so big I drown in it."

She sucked on him, drawing him deep into her throat, taking every last inch inside her.

She moved up and down his thick cock, her hand pumping him at the same time.

"*Gattra.* Crystal, you're so *xalta* sexy."

He groaned, then tensed and a flood of liquid filled her throat, pulsing into her. She swallowed, gulping to keep up with him. Never had a man filled her with so much.

Once he finished erupting inside her, she released him, then kissed up his stomach to his chest. To her total surprise, he rolled her onto her back and plunged into her again, his big cock still hard as steel.

Immediately, pleasure rocked through her. Her body quivered in sheer delight. He thrust again and again until finally she shrieked in ecstasy the world shattering around her.

He claimed her lips, drawing her firmly against his body. She snuggled against him, wondering how she'd slipped into orgasm so easily, especially without self-stimulation. That had never happened before. Ever since her first intimate relationship with her high-school sweetheart, which had been disappointing to say the least, her older sister had told her that the key to a great sex life for a woman was taking control of her own pleasure. Both Crystal and her sister had learned through their mother's experiences never to depend on a man and this was just another area where that was true.

After a few minutes of cuddling, she tried to ease away from his solid body, but he held her tight. She wanted to protest, wanted to slip into the other room and stretch out on her own bed, but the warmth of his body and the secure feeling of being in his arms lulled her, until the exhaustion of the day claimed her and she slipped into sleep.

Crystal awoke to find she couldn't move her arms and legs. She opened her eyes and realized that her wrists and ankles were bound with straps, her arms above her head and her legs stretched wide open. The bonds looked flimsy and felt silky against her skin, but they held her firm.

So the man was into bondage. This could be fun.

"They don't allow you to move, so you can't hurt yourself pulling against them."

Terrien stood in the doorway smiling at her, his gaze wandering over her completely naked body. Heat welled through her.

"I can position your limbs any way I want." He walked to the bed and lifted one of her arms then let go of it a few inches above the bed and it simply stayed there.

She felt no discomfort. Her arm just seemed to float, defying gravity.

"The bands have anti-grav built in. If I put the waistband on you, I could suspend you in midair."

She could imagine floating in front of him, at just the right height for his big cock to glide into her.

His gaze drifted to her open thighs and his forest green eyes darkened to almost black with golden glints like fireflies shimmering in their depths. Excitement skittered through her at the feel of being wide open to his heated gaze. He could touch her anywhere he wanted. And, God, she wanted him to touch her.

"So what are you going to do now?" she asked.

He eased her elevated arm back to rest on the bed and pressed her wrists together above her head, then his lips turned up in a devilish grin.

"Now, I'm going to show you how to receive pleasure."

CHAPTER 6

Crystal had done the bondage thing before and knew it didn't really work for her. If she couldn't access her clit, then the pleasure wouldn't come. But why challenge him? She couldn't decide if she'd fake an orgasm for him or if she should just let it go to show his arrogant self that she knew what she was talking about.

She watched as he stripped off his uniform. The sight of his broad shoulders and tight abs sent her heartbeat racing. Then he dropped his pants, revealing his impressive cock, already fully erect.

He knelt on the bed, then prowled over her, the hot flesh of his cock brushing against her belly. God, she ached for that monster inside her.

But it wouldn't take her anywhere. Not if he wouldn't let her touch herself.

He was so gorgeous, though, and so sweet for wanting to sweep her away with passion that she thought she'd be nice and fake it for him.

Except memories of being swept away last night after their first time, of actually plummeting into orgasm without any self-stimulation, threw her off a little. Had that happened because she'd been so primed and had just experienced the best orgasm of her life with him? Was what she'd felt that second time—and third—just an echo or continuation of the first orgasm?

His lips nuzzled her neck and her body pulsed with need. The thoughts drifted away. He nibbled her earlobe and then he kissed along her collarbone. Soon his tongue explored her body, starting with her shoulders, then gliding downward. Her nipples puckered and thrust forward as he lapped at the borders of her areolas but never broached the pebbling skin. He dabbed into her navel, then traveled downward, but curved around her pussy to her sensitive inner thighs.

Downward he continued, kissing her feet, then nipping the tips of her toes. He massaged her feet, relaxing her until she was absolutely boneless. She cooed as he stroked up her calves, back to her inner thighs. The sensual pleasure of his lips and massaging fingers stroking along her vulnerable flesh, especially with her legs splayed helplessly wide, sent strands of sensual delight threading through her.

She arched her pelvis, wanting him to touch her moist opening. He laughed but skimmed past her curls and moved upward. A moment later, his lips found her mouth, his tongue spearing inside her. She sucked on it, wanting it deep inside her. He cupped her face and stroked down her temple along her jawline as he kissed her. She breathed in his musky, male scent, longing for his body to merge with hers.

He released her lips, then kissed her neck and down her chest. He licked the edge of her aureola again, but this time continued over the nubby flesh until he circled her nipple, the tip of his tongue swirling around the tight bead.

"Oh, that feels so good."

She arched, pushing her breast farther into his mouth, her nipple buried in his warmth. He sucked, and she cried out at the glorious sensations bursting through her. He moved to the other nipple, his mouth escalating her desire. He lavished wonderful attention on both her breasts, from soft strokes of his fingertips to drawing her deep into his mouth and laving her rigid flesh to astonishing need.

Her vaginal muscles clenched, wanting him inside her.

"Terrien. Do it now."

"Do what, my love?"

At his somber, forest green gaze, she bit back her intended command to fuck her. He wanted more from her and she needed him enough to give it to him.

"Make love to me."

He smiled and shifted over her. She felt his deliciously rigid cock press against her flesh. Her breath caught in her lungs as he eased forward, sliding into her at an excruciatingly slow pace. She waited for him, quelling the urge to arch forward. He kissed her neck, just below her ear. A quiver of delightful sensation lit her nerve endings from her neck to the tips of her breasts. She shivered as he drew her firmly into his arms, almost the full length of his cock buried inside her.

"Oh, you feel so wonderful." She nuzzled his neck, longing to kiss every part of him.

He surged forward. She moaned at the incredible pleasure. Her inner muscles tightened around him, squeezing his thick shaft. Groaning, he eased back and surged forward again. Her clit twitched, longing to be stimulated.

"Release my hands," she whispered in his ear.

"No," he murmured hoarsely, his breath sending tendrils of hair fluttering across her neck.

He surged forward and drew back slowly. She moaned at the feel of his immense cock stretching her. Then he plunged deep again. She felt dizzy as waves of delight washed through her. He glided back and plunged deep again. She arched her pelvis against him, longing to clutch his thick, muscular shoulders.

He pumped into her steadily now. The pleasure built within her, taking her to the very edge, where she hovered in excruciating need.

"Please, I'm so close. I don't want to lose it."

"You won't," he said with confidence.

The elusive orgasm welled closer, but then skittered away.

"I *will*." Her whole body was stiff with anticipation mixed with frustration, sure that the prize would slip away.

He kissed her temple and thrust deep.

"You won't. Trust me, my love."

He shifted his hips and spiraled inside her. A thrilling sensation swirled through her, drawing the orgasm closer... Closer...

She groaned as it remained just out of reach. Every muscle in her body tensed, grasping for that elusive burst of pleasure.

"Just let go." His hand slid behind her and stroked her lower back.

His soothing touch was pure magic. The tension drained from her and her muscles relaxed, while the pleasure continued building in her as he surged his long, hard cock in and out of her hot, wet passage. Incredibly, she felt the elusive "O" approach, then ignite around the edges of her consciousness.

"Oh, God, oh, God, oh, GOD!"

She was consumed by an intoxicating flame of pure ecstasy. She rode the wave of passion as his cock penetrated her to the core, her body bouncing beneath him, pummeled with pure bliss.

He exploded within her, sending her over the top again.

Just as the second orgasm ebbed, he rocked his pelvis, then pivoted sideways, propelling her into another orgasm.

Her body vibrated in joyful pleasure. Time melted away as the euphoria claimed her totally.

Finally, she collapsed on the bed, gasping for breath.

"You see? I am able to bring you an orgasm without you needing to pleasure yourself."

He was right. He had brought her to orgasm, something a man had never done before, not without her help. Not just once but several times. And it was the most amazing pleasure she'd ever experienced in her life.

But…what if it was just a fluke? Last night might have been just because she'd been so primed, over such a long period of time. And this morning… What if that was just… luck? What if she never experienced anything like that again?

"It wasn't luck, Crystal," he said as if reading her mind.

To prove his point, he glided forward, sliding his cock into her again. Then he barely moved, just a slight vibration of his hips and she wailed as intense, bubbling pleasure crashed over her.

She gasped, hovering on the crest of the gigantic wave, then the orgasm surged through her. The world shattered around her and she moaned long and loud. When the pleasure slowed a little, he spiraled his hips and it exploded again. She screamed in pure ecstasy.

His lips drifted along her shoulder in butterfly kisses as he slowed his movements, releasing her from his sexual spell. She gasped in air, awash in amazement.

He brushed his lips on hers lightly, then smiled down at her, looking more satisfied than a man had a right to. Except, in his case, he did have that right after what he'd just given her.

She gazed at his face and the loving look in his eyes and somehow she knew it would be like that with him every time. He had a power over her. She shuddered at the thought, yet she still had an overwhelming need for closeness. The strange vulnerability frightened her, but at this moment, she was a slave to its demand.

"Hold me."

"Of course, sweetheart."

He released her bonds and wrapped his arms around her, drawing her close to his body. She curled up in his embrace, wanting the comfort of his touch, even though a part of her insisted it was his touch that frightened her.

She didn't like anyone having power over her. The more he gave her such pleasure, the more she would want it, then need it. It would become an addiction.

She couldn't allow that.

Crystal awoke in Terrien's arms. She opened her eyes and glanced around, a little disoriented. It felt like it should be morning, but it was dark in the room, with the exception of soft, artificial light.

"What time is it?" she asked.

"It's eleven-thirty in the morning your time," Terrien said.

She pushed herself onto her elbows. Black sky and a field of stars were visible through the small window on the wall to the left of the bed. It was forever night aboard this ship. Always artificial light. No sunshine. This would take some getting used to.

She sighed. "I usually do a morning run in the park."

"Well, we could go to the gym or how about a swim?"

"A swim? You have a pool aboard this ship?"

"Sure. We also have a river."

She laughed. "A river? I'd like to see that."

He kissed her, then pushed himself out of bed. She

couldn't help admiring his muscular physique, especially his long, dangling penis, remembering the pleasure it had given her.

"I'll make you some breakfast first. Ham and cheese omelet, right?"

"How did you know?" she asked.

He smiled. "I learned everything I could about you."

After breakfast, Crystal glanced at the choice of bathing suits Terrien showed her on a video screen. She chose a sexy black bikini with a floral sarong and he pressed a button, then walked to a wall compartment, slid open a door and pulled out the neatly folded garments. She felt odd walking through the corridor of the spaceship in a bikini and sheer sarong, but the crew they passed, all in uniform, paid little attention except for the appreciative glances of a few of the men as they gazed at her ample show of bosom.

"It's here." Terrien turned toward a door and it slid open.

As she followed him through the doorway, she felt as if they were walking outdoors.

She stepped onto grass and walked past bushes as she gazed upward to see a blue sky, a few light, fluffy clouds and what appeared to be the sun.

"Wow. The sun and sky look so real. I assume this is some kind of virtual reality thing."

"Unfortunately we don't technology as advanced as represented in your science fiction yet. The water is real and flows around the circumference of the ship. The illusion of the natural setting is achieved with holograms. The river isn't huge, but it's pleasant to relax on a floater while the water carries you around or you can swim against the current to get a good workout."

Crystal glanced at the river, which was about eight feet wide, surrounded by sandy beach. She took off her sandals, then stepped onto the soft, fine sand. It was warm and squished between her toes. She laughed at the sensual feel of it.

There were lounge chairs along the river, some occupied by other people. Terrien took her hand and led her toward a couple of free chairs a few feet from the water's edge. She unfastened the sarong and pushed it into the beach bag Terrien had brought with them, then grabbed a towel from inside and draped it over the chair. She stretched out, soaking in the pleasant feel of the sun warming her skin.

She glanced around at the other people. Some wore bathing suits and others were completely naked. Most were just relaxing, but one couple was in a passionate embrace, while another had removed their swimsuits and were exploring each other's bodies.

"Your people certainly seem to be comfortable with their sexuality. Unless this is a ship of perverts."

He laughed. "No, this is pretty typical. There are appropriate and inappropriate places for sexual activity, but we're not as restrictive as on your world. Public sexuality is fine in appropriate places."

"Like beaches and swimming pools?"

"We also have lounges and clubs for such things. We have a special recreation room on the ship, called the Red Room, where people can enjoy each other sexually or watch others. Voyeurism is an accepted activity."

"Hmm." Her nipples puckered as she watched the couple five chairs away stroking each other.

The man's hand slipped between the woman's legs and his fingers glided inside her. She moaned, her hands stroking over his tight, naked buttocks, his cock swelling against her thighs.

"I'm going in the water," Crystal announced, knowing if she watched much longer, she'd be jumping Terrien's bones.

She stood up and walked across the sand, then stepped into the river. The water was a lovely temperature, eighty-five or so. Terrien grabbed some floater pads from a stack by the bushes and followed her. He handed her one and they both settled on them and allowed the gentle current to pull them along.

"You aren't worried about our bag?" she asked as she watched their lounge chairs disappear in the distance.

"No. It'll still be there when we get back."

He looked so relaxed, stretched out on the mat with his eyes closed. She gazed at his gorgeous body, his sculpted muscles beaded with water droplets glistening in the sunlight. She settled back, too, enjoying the gentle buoying of the water as it carried them away.

After about twenty minutes, they returned to their lounge chairs. The couple who had been going at it were gone, but another couple nearby was well into foreplay. The woman's head bobbed up and down on the man's ample cock as she crouched beside him and he fingered her naked pussy. Crystal did her best to ignore them, even though the sight of the big cock gliding into her mouth made Crystal crave the same thing.

She lay back on the chair and closed her eyes, enjoying the warm feel of the simulated sunshine on her body. At the gentle brush of lips on her stomach, she opened her eyes.

"What are you doing?" she asked Terrien.

He tugged on the tie on one side of her bikini bottom, releasing the bow. She clamped her hand down on it.

"I don't think so."

He grinned. "Well, as long as you're not sure."

He tugged free the other bow.

CHAPTER 7

Crystal whisked his hands away and refastened the ties.

"Oh, I'm quite sure."

He kissed the swell of her breast. "Why not? Wouldn't it be exciting to know people were watching you?"

A shiver of excitement rushed through her and she glanced around. The other couple was now in full swing, the man thrusting into the attractive brunette beneath him. Another couple nearby was in a passionate embrace, also fully naked. Other people were watching them with avid interest.

Her gaze returned to the nearer couple, her heart pounding as the man pounded into the woman.

Crystal's groin clenched. She wanted Terrien again. Right now.

"I..." She shook her head, unsure why she hesitated. Seeing the other couples enjoying each other sent an erotic charge through her and the thought of people watching her as she indulged in sexual play was a turn on.

But not with Terrien. When she was with him, she wanted it to be...private. Intimate.

He watched her face and smiled as if reading her thoughts. He leaned forward and kissed her, his lips moving on hers with a gentle pressure. Her arms slid around his neck, and she pulled him closer, deepening the kiss. Her heart thundered and her insides melted with need.

He drew her to her feet, their lips never parting. Her breasts, crushed against his hard, muscular chest, swelled with need, her nipples pushing into him. He drew back and smiled.

"You said you like to run in the mornings. How fast can you make it back to our quarters?" he asked with a grin.

She picked up the towel she'd been lying on, then tossed it at his face.

"Faster than you." She turned and dodged to the door, laughing.

He swept up her sandals and the beach bag, then raced after her, the towel fluttering behind him as he ran. She dodged past the few people she encountered in the corridor, laughing and running until she reached his door only seconds before him. The door slid open, and they practically tumbled inside. He grabbed her and pulled her into his arms while the door slid closed behind them. His lips caressed hers with a gentle passion.

God, but the man could kiss. She stroked down his hard chest, then over his rippled abs until she reached the top of his swim trunks, her fingers itching to feel his big, solid cock in her hand. He stripped away his trunks as she grabbed on to his shaft and stroked. She dropped to her knees and wrapped her lips around his thick member, the mushroom head gliding into her mouth. She licked around, then nuzzled her tongue under the corona and teased as he groaned.

She stroked the kid-leather-soft flesh stretched over his iron shaft and sucked on him. Her insides ached with yearning to have him inside her, pumping deep and hard, driving her to scintillating joy. But more, she wanted to bring him pleasure and to experience that pleasure in a direct and primal way.

"Oh, come for me, baby," she said, then licked the tiny hole oozing clear liquid, her hands wrapped firmly around him while she continued stroking. "I want you to come in my mouth."

She took him deep again, and his fingers forked through her hair. He held her head within his big, warm hands.

"*Gattra*, woman. How can I resist?"

She stroked his tightening balls and sucked deeply, satisfaction spiking through her as he groaned again. She glided farther on his long shaft, taking him deep into her throat. Still he didn't climax.

She drew him from her mouth and licked his length. Glancing up, she saw his tight features. Damn it, he was holding back.

"If you aren't resisting, why aren't you coming?" She wanted him to come. She wanted to know she could give him as much pleasure as he gave her.

"Because I love what you're doing. I love that you want me." He stroked her hair tenderly. "I don't want it to end."

She grinned at him. "I'm going to give you exactly ten seconds. Come, or I walk away."

Without waiting for a response, she swallowed his cockhead and sucked—hard—then dove deep on him again. She spiraled her hands around the exposed part of his shaft while she bobbed up and down. Within a couple of heartbeats, his fingers tightened around her head and he groaned. Hot liquid spurted into her mouth, spilling out her lips before she could swallow it all. Still he kept erupting, as she gulped to keep up with him.

Finally, he relaxed. His shrunken cock slipped from her mouth.

She licked her lips and smiled at him. He took her hand and drew her to her feet, then kissed her. His tongue dove between her lips and his mouth consumed hers, his arms tightening around her to crush her tight to his body. Their hearts thumped together in unison.

"*Gattra*, woman. You are so *fakkreh* hot!"

"Mmm. You're pretty fakray hot yourself." She nuzzled under his chin as she wrapped her hand around his rising cock, but he swept her up and carried her into his bedroom.

He tossed her onto the bed and prowled over her. He stroked her thighs, pressing them wide. She felt her bikini bottoms slip away and his mouth burrow into her pussy with a vengeance. His tongue drove into her, then swept up to her clit as his fingers glided along her wet opening. Several pushed inside her. Before she could catch her breath, pleasure launched through her. She gasped, then released the air from her lungs as his fingers stretched her. He sucked her clit and she arched against his mouth.

"Oh, honey, that is *gattra* fucking sexy." She moaned.

He chuckled. "You've got the mouth of a sailor."

"And you have the mouth of a fucking saint." She grabbed his head and pushed it back to her wet flesh.

He dove in again with gusto, his tongue sweeping across her clit. His fingers moved inside her, stroking and twirling, then pulsing deep. The orgasm catapulted through her in a sudden spike. She gasped, then moaned as the pleasure blazed through her, singeing every nerve ending.

Finally, she flopped back against the pillows, totally spent.

"I think you enjoyed that." Terrien stretched out beside her, a satisfied smile on his face.

She rolled on top of him and grabbed his shoulders, then devoured his mouth, tasting herself on his lips.

"You *think?*" She squeezed his thick thighs between hers, feeling his bulge pressing against her. She shifted until it was in the ideal position to stimulate her clit. "If you know me as well as you seem to, I would think you'd *know*."

He grabbed her shoulders and flipped her onto her back, then rolled her over again, until she was on the bed on her stomach. He climbed on top of her, nudged her legs apart with his knees, then glided his cock over her moist opening and pushed the shaft tight against her clit.

She groaned, echoes of her recent orgasm vibrating along her nerve endings. He drew her hips upward, then pressed his cockhead against her slit and glided inside. She sucked in air as his big cock filled her.

"There's something I know you'd like that we haven't done yet." He pushed in and out a couple of times, then withdrew, to her disappointed whimper.

When she felt his big cock nudge against her back opening, she stiffened.

"Oh, wait. I've certainly taken some serious cock back there, but honey, I'm afraid you might just be too much for me."

He kissed the back of her neck. "Don't worry. Remember, I'm not like the men you've been with before. I have different abilities."

His cockhead pushed against her and…it seemed to shrink. He pushed forward and her opening stretched around him, but he slipped inside easily.

"What's happening?"

"I can change the size of my penis. I've made it smaller so I won't hurt you."

He glided deeper, lubricated by the moisture from her vagina.

"Really? Not a direction you'd think a woman would want, but…"

He barely stretched her as he slid inside.

"Oh, God, that feels so good."

He pushed deep, then paused. His hand stroked around her hip, then down her belly until his fingers stroked over her curls. He found her clit and she sighed. As he plucked at her sensitive nub, she shifted back, pushing his cock a little deeper.

"Are you ready for a little more?" he asked.

She nodded, not quite sure what he was suggesting but ready for whatever this talented man had in mind. Then his shaft grew…slowly…stretching her back passage.

"Oh, yes." Wild pangs of sensation darted through her, and her insides felt so full, she thought she'd burst. But not too full. He stopped before he reached his full breadth, then he began to pump into her.

She gasped, her heart thundering as every cell in her body tingled in delight. He stroked her clit with his thumb as his fingers pushed into her slick vagina.

"Oh, yes." She threw her head back against his shoulder. "Oh, God."

His lips nuzzled the side of her neck as ecstasy catapulted through her and she wailed in delight. He pumped and stroked. His cock grew wider and her joy intensified. She gasped, then nearly fainted as the pleasure washed her away to a primal sea of pure bliss.

When the orgasm finally waned, he held her tight to his body as she gasped for air.

They both slumped on the pillow. He kissed her neck and rolled them both sideways, still holding her tight to him.

"Crystal, *laiya*, I love you," he murmured in her ear.

Crystal stiffened in his arms. Oh, God, she did not want him to love her.

CHAPTER 8

Terrien ached inside as Crystal pulled away from him.

"Look, honey, the sex is great and all," she said, "but let's get one thing straight right now. I don't believe in soul-mates and I don't want you to love me. I am definitely not the one-man woman type."

"Crystal, how can you not believe in soul-mates now that you have experienced what we have together?"

Her beautiful, full lips turned down in a frown. "Look, I admit the sex is sensational." She shrugged. "But that's all it is. Sex." She paced. "I mean, I like you. And we have fun together. But I'm not going to give up my freedom because you and I are great in the sack."

Terrien's heart ached. All his life he'd known he would eventually find his soul-mate, the one woman who would love him forever. Completely and unconditionally. That thought had carried him through many difficult times. Especially after his parents' deaths when he was nine years old. His uncle and aunt raised him, but they had their own children and as much as they clearly loved him, it was not the same as it had been with his own mother and father. To them he had been special. He had been *their* son.

When he'd first felt the gnawing awareness of his soulmate, he'd rejoiced. He'd felt like he would truly belong to someone again. Someone meant specifically for him.

And if it had been a woman from *Sa'oul* then everything would have been fine. She would have understood about *tanash'aei*. She would have loved him without question. But he'd been connected to an Earth woman. Someone who resisted the whole concept of linked souls.

Not that he wished his *tanash'ae* was someone different. How could he? He loved Crystal with all his being. But it hurt more than anyone could fathom that she rejected him.

"Terrien, I'm sorry. It's just...the way I am. I live my own life. Not depending on anyone else. No one else depending on me. I don't even have a cat."

She'd rather be alone than be with him? His heart shuddered in agony.

But he drew in a deep breath, reminding himself she had been dragged into this whole situation a matter of days ago. She needed time to get used to the idea. Right now, she was justifying her fear of what she didn't understand.

He would not give up hope. He needed to be patient while she adapted to the situation.

Maybe if he learned more about her life and her culture, it would help. Reading about it and viewing their entertainment could take him only so far.

"What do you mean, you don't have a cat?" He knew a cat was a small furry animal with a tail and pointed ears. The creatures spent time with humans, but he didn't know what she meant by *having* a cat.

"A cat. You know, it's a pet."

"Pet? You mean animals that cohabit a community with humans?"

"Um, yeah, I guess. But it's more that a cat cohabits a house with someone. A pet *belongs* to someone."

Belongs? "You mean, people *own* animals?"

"Yeah, sure. Don't you have pets on your planet?"

"We have animals that are friendly and affectionate with humans. Often they will attach to an individual or family, but they roam free and we never think of them as owned by anyone."

"Oh, well. It's different on Earth. At least, where I'm from. When someone gets a pet, they keep it in their house and feed and care for it. People get pretty attached to their pets."

"But not you."

She shook her head. "No. I don't want to depend on anyone and I don't want anyone depending on me."

At her words, his chest clenched. How could she not understand that *tanash'aei* did depend on each other? For pleasure. For happiness. For love.

But that was the problem. She did understand.

And she rejected the whole concept.

Terrien sat across from Larson as they ate their lunch. He and Larson had been friends for several years, even before Larson had been promoted to the rank of commander. They both had a duty shift today and were taking their break together.

"You know, I learned something new about the Earth women's culture yesterday," Terrien said. "Crystal told me about pets. It seems that people own animals like cats as companions and they become quite attached to them."

"Really?"

"They keep them in their houses rather than allowing them to roam free."

Larson frowned. "So I assume these pets rely on their owners." He tapped on the table with his fingertips. "I wonder if any of the women we brought here has a pet."

"I know Crystal doesn't, but I don't know about the others."

"I didn't see anything in Eva's file, either, but I'll check the other women's. We wouldn't want to cause a problem because of separating someone from their pet."

It was a valid point. Although some of the women had family left behind on Earth, the family were all grown people who had lives of their own. A pet, on the other hand, was a dependent of sorts and the tie would be different.

Terrien took a bite of food, although he wasn't really hungry. He still ached inside at Crystal's rejection.

"So how is Eva adapting to the idea of being here?" Terrien asked.

Larson put down his fork and stared at Terrien. He could see his own pain mirrored in Larson's eyes.

Larson shook his head. "Not well." His hand tightened into a fist and his jaw clenched. "I don't understand it. How can she feel the intense craving we have for each other and not know the truth of our connection?"

Terrien shook his head at his friend's words, echoing his own dilemma. Although he didn't wish this difficulty on his friend, it helped Terrien to know he wasn't the only one experiencing a problem with his *tanash'ae*. That made him feel less alone.

Of course, he should not doubt the wisdom of *nata'tai*, but sometimes even the most faithful had doubts. At least now he knew he had someone he could talk to about it. Someone who would understand.

"Is it the same with you and Crystal?" Larson asked.

Terrien nodded. "She says she does not want to share her life with someone."

"Have you"—Larson stared at his plate—"consummated your relationship yet?"

Terrien stared at Larson and, from the set of his jaw, realized Larson had not.

Gattra, the man must be going insane. Terrien couldn't imagine being so close to his *tanash'ae* for so long without consummating.

"Yes, we have, but Crystal seems more open about sex than is typical for Earth women."

Larson nodded, but they both knew that with the connection urging *tanash'aei* to be together, even a shy Earth woman would be consumed with need. Terrien couldn't imagine how Larson's woman could resist her *tanash'ae*.

"If there's anything I can do to help…" Terrien said. "If you need to talk any time…just let me know."

It was little solace, but friendship was the best Terrien could offer.

Larson nodded. "And the same with you. If there's anything I can do to help, let me know."

Larson picked up his fork and began to eat again.

~

Crystal sat propped against the pillows on the bed staring at the e-reader, but the words blurred in front of her.

She'd learned long ago not to become dependent on anyone, especially a man. When her mother had gotten married young, probably pregnant with Crystal's older sister, she'd been disowned by her father, Crystal's grandfather. When Crystal's father died six years later, leaving Crystal's mom poverty stricken with two young daughters and no means of support, Crystal's grandfather had not relented.

So her mother had found she could not depend on her own father who should have cared about her, or her husband who should have helped her raise their children. Of course, Crystal's dad hadn't had a choice, but that just went to show that even when a guy is reliable, a woman shouldn't depend on him. Things happen.

And in her mother's case, she went on to a string of bad relationships. She'd fall in love with a guy, then wind up heartbroken and crying on Crystal's shoulder. It had been devastating to watch. Crystal had learned from her mother's situation and vowed never to allow herself to be so vulnerable. She would not depend on a man, or anyone else. Ever.

She heard the door to the quarters open. It would be Terrien returning from his shift. She set the e-reader on the table beside her bed and stood up. As she walked out of her bedroom and through his, she steeled herself for the conversation to come.

She didn't want to hurt him, but she had to make him understand that she did not intend be in a monogamous relationship with him. Just because he believed in soulmates, it didn't mean she did and she had to make it clear that she would not have him force his beliefs on her and her life.

The thing that threw her off so completely was Terrien's ability to give her such astonishing pleasure. She needed to know if this was unique to Terrien or if any of the alien men could do it.

As she stepped into the living room, he glanced up and smiled.

"Hello." He walked toward her.

A yearning grew inside her with every step he took. When he drew her into his arms and his solid body pressed against her, need shimmered through her. His lips captured hers with such tenderness and passion, she melted against him.

Oh, God, the man knew how to kiss.

But the longing was too powerful. It overwhelmed and frightened her, so she reached deep inside herself for the strength to draw away.

"Is there something wrong?" he asked as she stepped back.

"We need to talk."

"All right. I'd like to learn more about your culture and—"

"Not about that." She took his hand and led him to the couch.

Most men would have cringed at her remark, since it was generally a precursor to a relationship talk, but Terrien was from another world and didn't have the same triggers as human men.

She sat down and he sat beside her.

"What do you want to talk about?" he asked.

"Well, you've been a wonderful host, but I'd like to experience something new."

"New?" His eyebrows drew together. "But haven't most of the things you've experienced here been new to you?"

"Yes, that's true, but I've only been here with you and as great as things have been between us, I'd like to..." She hesitated, not quite finding it in herself to be as direct as she usually was. She shrugged. "Um, well, I'd like to see someone else."

"See?" His eyes narrowed. "Exactly what are you trying to say?"

She sighed. "Okay, here it is. I'm on a ship of aliens. You've already proven that you have interesting abilities. And I told you I'm not a one-man woman."

His hands balled into fists and his warm gaze cooled, glinting with a hard edge.

"Are you actually saying you want to be with another man?"

His sharp tone threw her off. She stood up and started to pace.

"Look, I've never pretended to be something I'm not. I like being with men and I never stay with one for very long. That's just how I am." She stopped and faced him, meeting his hard gaze. "I won't apologize for who I am."

"And I won't apologize for who I am. Or what I believe in. You are my soul-mate and soul-mates don't go off with other lovers."

She planted her hands on her hips. "But I don't believe in soul-mates and I do whatever I damned well please."

He stood up and stepped toward her, his height and irate demeanor a little intimidating. "I forbid it. I will not allow my *tanash'ae* to have sex with another man."

Anger flared though her. "Are you saying I'm your prisoner?"

"No, you're my *tanash'ae*."

"If that means you get to control my life, then from what I'm hearing, there's no difference. Are you going to keep me locked up in these quarters for the rest of the trip? And when we arrive on your planet, will you keep me locked up in your house?"

He scowled. "Of course not. You're not a prisoner."

"So I can come and go as I please?"

His jaw twitched. "Yes, of course."

"So how are you going to stop me from having sex with other men?"

"Now it's other *men*?" Anger flared in his eyes again.

She ignored the comment and strode toward the door. "You mentioned there's a special lounge where people can go to have sex. I'm sure I'll find someone there who'll want to be with me."

CHAPTER 9

Crystal's heart pounded as she strode toward the door.

"Crystal, wait."

She turned to glare at him. "Are you going to stop me?"

He hesitated, his lips compressed in a straight line, but finally he shook his head. "No, but I'm asking you not to go."

As soon as she opened her mouth to protest, he shook his head.

"Don't go to the Red Room. If you really want to..." He frowned, his hands clenching and unclenching. "If you really want to have sex with someone else, let me set it up."

Her eyes narrowed. "Why would you do that?"

She hardened her heart to the pain lancing across his face.

"Because I don't think you should be with just anyone. I think you should be with someone who understands your culture. And who speaks your language. Not everyone on the ship does."

What he said made sense.

"Okay."

It felt weird that he was going to set her up with someone, but this was good. It showed that he was willing to face the fact that she would not be his one-and-only. Because she refused to be in a monogamous relationship with any man. She valued her freedom far too much.

Even though being with Terrien held a stronger appeal than she dared to admit.

∼

Terrien walked along the corridor, his heart aching. He wanted Crystal to be his and his alone, but the woman just wouldn't accept that. It was killing him inside knowing she wanted to be with another man, that he couldn't satisfy her enough to keep her happy.

Dahran, how could she want to be with someone else? She was meant to be with him. And he with her.

He stepped into the lounge and saw Larson sitting at a table waiting, a drink in front of him. Terrien walked to the bar and ordered a drink too, then carried it to the table.

"You look like you need a friend," Larson said as Terrien sat down.

Terrien took a sip, then nodded. "I have a favor to ask and it's a strange one."

"Is it about Crystal?"

Terrien nodded and wrapped his fingers around the glass. "I'll understand if you say no, especially since you have your own *tanash'ae* to deal with."

"Just ask."

"Crystal wants to have sex with another man."

Larson frowned. "You're not okay with this, so why are you asking?"

Terrien sighed. "She's very headstrong and she doesn't believe in soul-mates. I think this is her way of proving to herself that what she and I have is not special. I think she feels that maybe another alien man will satisfy her needs."

Larson grinned, relieving the tension a little. "So you want me to disappoint her?"

Terrien chuckled. "No. I want you to give her the ride of her life. Then she'll see it's not just about the pleasure a man can give her. She'll see that being with a soul-mate is a deeper experience."

Larson grabbed Terrien's shoulder and squeezed, an acknowledgment of their shared pain. Then he nodded.

"Seriously, I am willing to help, but I must warn you, I will tell Eva that I intend to be with another woman. That will force her to question how she truly feels about me and our relationship. I will also tell her that if she asks me not to go forward with this, then I won't."

"I understand and I hope for your sake that she does protest, but for my own sake, I hope she does not."

Larson nodded. "So let's see where *nata'tai* takes us."

Crystal walked beside Terrien down the corridor, her heart accelerating. This was really happening. Terrien was delivering her to another man's quarters. For sex.

"It's here," he said as he stopped in front of a door.

They waited patiently. Crystal assumed some kind of sensor informed the occupant of the quarters that they were outside. She smoothed her dress over her hips as they waited. Terrien had created a copy of the red evening gown she'd been wearing when she first came aboard the ship. The one Terrien had torn off her during their first frantic sexual encounter. The memory of that night still took her breath away.

In fact, the memory of every sexual encounter with Terrien took her breath away.

Terrien glanced at her and she could tell he noticed her

peaked nipples pushing at the thin fabric of the dress. From the tight set of his jaw, he probably thought her arousal was in anticipation of the sexual tryst ahead of her. In truth, she actually felt a little nervous. What if this man didn't live up to Terrien's prowess? What if he was as good as Terrien, but she still didn't climax without self-stimulation?

The door slid open and she glanced up to see the handsome Commander Raa-ling. He was incredibly hot and sexy. She was also pretty sure he was Eva's man, yet Terrien said that soul-mates don't have sex with other people.

"Good evening." He smiled at her, revealing even white teeth in a dazzling smile.

Her lips turned up. "Good evening, Commander."

"Please call me Larson," he said as she stepped into his quarters, which were a little bigger than Terrien's but essentially the same.

The door closed and when she glanced behind her, Terrien was gone. Well, of course, he wouldn't come in and join them on her...date. Though the thought of both Terrien and Larson giving her pleasure at the same time sent thrills through her. Maybe that's what she should have suggested. Maybe Terrien would have found that more palatable.

As soon as she realized her thoughts were turning to how to adapt her needs to Terrien's, she cut them off. This was about what *she* needed. Terrien was not really her soul-mate. He had no claim on her.

No, it was better this way. A threesome including Terrien would not make the point she needed to with him.

"Would you like a drink?" Larson asked.

She nodded and he picked up a red bottle and poured a clear liquid into a tall glass and handed it to her. She took a sip. It had a delicate fruit flavor, like berries and a little citrus. She took another sip and warmth spread through her, relaxing her.

Larson was tall and sexy, with a muscular body and long honey-gold hair hanging loose around his shoulders. His stunning turquoise eyes filled with heat as he watched her. Her gaze slid to his full, sensual mouth, then down to his big hands.

Her insides throbbed with need. She was anxious to experience his touch, to see if he could bring her as much pleasure as Terrien could.

She smiled and walked toward him, her gaze running the length of his body, up and down. In response, he openly surveyed her body, sending her nipples rising again. He smiled and stepped forward, his gaze settling on the swell of her bosom. She glanced at his crotch and the healthy-sized bulge forming there.

Did all these alien guys have huge cocks? If so, this planet they were going to could be quite the place to visit.

She tipped back her glass and finished the drink, then smiled enticingly. "I assume the bedroom is this way?"

He led her to what she presumed was the bedroom door.

She stepped into the room, then walked toward the big bed. She could feel Larson behind her. She turned around and slid her hands over his broad shoulders, then around his thick neck. The heat in his eyes flared and he lowered his mouth to hers.

His lips moved expertly on hers and her body melted against him. Oh, God, he was hot. Excitement blazed through her at the warm pressure of his mouth, the gentle caress of his tongue, the heady male taste of him. She stroked his neck and the back of his head, her fingers forking through his long, honey-colored hair.

Her heartbeat accelerated and her breasts swelled. Tingles danced along her skin as she anticipated the feel of his hands exploring her body.

His mouth moved passionately on hers, arousing her in a

way no kiss ever had before. She clung to his shoulders for support, her knees turning rubbery. She arched against him and moaned. His hands stroked over her back, pulling her closer against his hard, muscular body.

"Oh, my God, what you're doing to me…" Crystal voice was hoarse with need. "I mean, you really know how to—"

Larson pulled her against him again, driving his tongue into her mouth. His hand glided down her back and cupped her ass. She arched against him, thrilled at the feel his rock-hard cock against her.

Her insides ached with yearning and she moaned as a sweet euphoria vibrated through her. It swelled within her and…

Oh, God. She gasped as she undulated against him, then groaned into his mouth as her body quivered in erotic bliss. The orgasm, catching her totally off guard, shimmered through her.

Finally, she slumped in his arms, stunned. Their lips parted and Crystal stared up at him, wide-eyed.

"My God, that was fabulous." Crystal's voice was breathless.

She gazed into his vivid turquoise eyes and smiled. If this man could bring her to orgasm with just a kiss, what else was in store for her this evening?

CHAPTER 10

Crystal unzipped her dress and dropped it to the floor. Her nipples, hard and thrusting forward, peeked out over her red lace demi-bra. She felt exceptionally sexy as Larson's gaze wandered over her mostly naked breasts with an appreciative glint in his eyes. Crystal rested her hands on his solid shoulders and ran her fingers downward to the buttons, then she unfastened them one by one. She pushed the fabric aside and admired his broad, sculpted chest.

She ran her hand across his hard muscles and leaned forward to lick his nipple, then drew it into her mouth. The pearl-hard bud rolled against her tongue.

Larson's hand stroked over her hip and the lacy strap of her matching thong panties. Her heart rate increased as his warm finger slid under the strap and started to move forward. She reached around behind her and released her bra, then dropped it to the floor. Larson's gaze locked on her breasts, her pink nipples jutting forward. He stroked one and she quivered.

He leaned down and took the stiff nipple into his mouth. She murmured at the delicious sensation, then offered him the other. He nibbled and sucked for several moments. Her breasts ached and her insides melted in need. As the pleasure swelled within her, she gasped. He sucked again, hard, and her breath caught. Oh, God, she was close to coming again. She wrapped her hands around his head and pulled him tighter against her breast. His hot, wet mouth moved on her, shifting from one breast to the other, until the scintillating sensations exploded through her. She moaned on a long, ecstatic note as an orgasm tore through her.

She gasped for air as her heart rate slowly returned to normal. Well, she'd certainly had no reason to worry about whether Terrien was the only one who could bring her to orgasm without her help. Larson seemed more than capable. God, he was absolutely brilliant.

But she still couldn't stop thinking about Terrien. Wishing it was Terrien who was touching her now. Tasting her.

Holding her.

But she smiled. "Honey, you are exceptionally talented."

She pushed aside her thoughts of Terrien, or at least tried to, and stripped off her panties, then arranged herself on the bed in an artfully sexy pose, her hands behind her head. Smiling, she sent Larson a come-hither look.

He approached the bed slowly, his gaze gliding over her sexy body.

"Do you like someone watching you, Crystal?"

Watching? Was Terrien watching them? But no, it wouldn't be him, because she was sure that Terrien would not want to see her receiving pleasure from another man. So he must mean someone else.

As she thought about it, she realized the idea of someone watching them did turn her on. She hadn't wanted that with Terrien, but with Larson, she could relax and enjoy her natural inclination.

"Mmm. Is someone watching us?" Crystal stroked her nipples with her fingertips.

"Eva, come on in," Larson called, his gaze never straying from Crystal's naked body.

"Eva?" Crystal sat forward, her eyes widening and a smile curled her lips. "Where is she?"

Larson's head nudged toward an open door on the other side of the bedroom. Crystal got up and walked into the other room where she saw Eva sitting on the edge of her bed wearing a red velour robe. Eva's gaze darted from a video screen to Crystal.

Crystal pivoted around to see what Eva had been watching and saw a view of Larson tossing his pants aside and lying on his bed. His enormous cock stood straight up. And the thought of that cock driving into her stole her breath away, especially after experiencing how very talented this man was with his equipment.

"Oh, you naughty thing." Crystal grabbed Eva's hand and pulled her to her feet, giving her a big hug. "I'm glad you're okay. Is this guy your tannashay?"

Eva shifted uncomfortably. "So he tells me."

"And you're willing to share him?" Crystal was immensely glad she was.

Eva shrugged. "I don't believe in the soul-mate relationships."

"Yeah, I know what you're saying." Crystal tugged Eva forward and led her to the other room. "Doesn't mean we can't enjoy the situation, though."

Crystal stopped and admired the naked man in front of them. "What an incredible cock, don't you think?"

Eva stared at it—tall, hard and purple-headed—and nodded.

"Since you're willing to share him with me, why don't *I* share him with *you*?" Crystal suggested.

It would be fun sharing this man with Eva. And it made Crystal feel less alone, having not only another woman along for the ride, but an Earth woman. Crystal hadn't realized how much she'd started to feel isolated from home.

Eva looked a little confused. She'd probably never had a threesome before.

"Oh, come on. You've probably been making love with him nonstop. I would have been."

Eva shook her head. The way she avoided Crystal's gaze and the slight flush to her cheeks made Crystal wonder.

"You mean, you haven't? At all?"

"Not exactly," Eva responded.

Larson smiled. "Only the time she tied me up and had her way with me."

Eva? Into bondage?

Crystal grinned. "Oh, kinky. I love it. Well, come on, let's both give him head."

Eva's eyes widened at Crystal's suggestion and she stared at Larson's erection, but hesitated.

"Okay, honey, you watch and join in anytime," Crystal said.

Crystal sat on the side of the bed and wrapped her hand around his thick cock, then leaned down and licked it from base to tip. The feel of the soft skin stretched over a rock-hard shaft sent her insides quivering. She lapped to his tip, then drew him into her mouth. His girth stretched her jaw wide as she slid her lips down, then up his ample erection. Ripples of need pulsed through her as Larson moaned appreciatively.

God, if he was having this effect on her, what must Eva be experiencing, since she had an actual link to the man?

Crystal tensed and had to force herself not to pause. God, what was wrong with her? She couldn't really be starting to believe in this tannashay stuff. Could she?

Her disturbing thoughts were interrupted by Eva sitting down on the opposite side of the bed. Crystal released Larson's cock from her mouth, then licked one side of the shaft. Eva leaned forward and licked the other side. Larson groaned.

Crystal reached toward Eva and untied the belt at her waist, then tugged open her robe, revealing her black lace bra beneath.

Eva hesitated, then stood and dropped her robe to the floor. Crystal smiled approvingly, then crawled toward Larson. His gaze lingered on Eva as his large hand stroked over Crystal's ass. Crystal leaned forward, nudging her breast toward Larson's lips. Intently watching Crystal's hard nub disappearing into Larson's mouth, Eva let her bra fall to the floor, then shed her panties.

Eva was a beautiful woman and Crystal watched her appreciatively. As did Larson, while he continued to lap and suck on Crystal's nipple with enthusiasm, sending tingles through her.

It was a real turn-on being here with this sexy hunk of man and another naked woman. Sharing his big cock with Eva.

After several moments, Crystal offered Larson her other breast. Eva's fingers stroked her own rigid nipples. Eva kneeled on the bed beside one of Larson's long, muscular thighs, watching.

Finally, Crystal sat back on her heels.

"Sweetie, don't forget Eva. She needs some of that wonderful tongue."

"I can't. I promised not to touch her unless she asks me to."

"Oh, really?" She smiled at Eva. "You like control." A woman after her own heart.

Crystal stroked down Eva's belly and across her slit. The flesh was hot and slick.

"Honey, you're way past ready. Tell him what you want. Don't let me being here stop you."

"No, I..."

Crystal couldn't understand Eva's hesitation. She hadn't had sex with the man and she was holding back now. Crystal didn't know what was going on between them, but Eva was here at her own free will and she obviously wanted the man.

"Okay, well, I didn't make any such promise," Crystal said.

CHAPTER 11

Crystal tumbled Eva down and climbed over her, dipping her tongue into Eva's slit, then dabbing the clitoris.

Eva's eyes widened. "No, I… Oh, God."

Crystal smiled. Just as she thought. Eva just needed a little encouragement. Maybe she could help these two get past whatever it was that was stopping them. She stroked Eva's nipple, ensuring it was nice and hard. Then stopped.

"Honey, do you want *me* to touch your breasts or Larson?"

Eva hesitated again, clearly struggling with her desire.

"Larson," she finally responded.

Crystal smiled. "Then tell him."

Larson sat up. The gentleness and need in his turquoise eyes melted her heart. God, the man was clearly in love with Eva.

"Do you want me to, sweetheart?" he murmured.

Eva nodded.

"Tell me," he whispered hoarsely.

"Please touch my breasts." Eva's breathy words were a mere whisper.

His hands covered her, stroking.

"Suck them," Eva pleaded.

He covered them with his mouth and she moaned. His tongue swirled around one tip, then the other. As he continued to suck, Eva wailed as a sudden orgasm washed over her.

Crystal sat back on her heels and smiled approvingly. Good for Eva.

"Why don't you ask him to lick your clit?" Crystal suggested.

Eva gazed at her man with half-lidded eyes.

"Larson, please kiss me down there."

"It's called a pussy, honey," Crystal offered.

He moved to Eva's intimate flesh, his tongue nudging into the folds, then flicked her clit. She moaned.

Crystal's insides ached with need. She settled under Larson's kneeling form and grasped his big cock, then sucked it deep into her mouth. Larson murmured approvingly as he continued to cajole Eva's intimate flesh. Eva arched and threw her head back, moaning in ecstasy. Crystal licked and sucked the big, hard cockhead filling her mouth.

Eva rocked against Larson's mouth as she coiled her fingers through his long hair, moaning his name.

"Oh, my God, Larson," Eva trilled. "You're making me... come."

His mouth and tongue stayed buried deep in her, lapping and teasing. Keeping her at the height of bliss.

Finally, Eva fell back against the bed and Larson stroked her breasts as Crystal continued sucking his hard flesh. He stiffened, his face contorting with pleasure, and he captured Eva's lips as he erupted in orgasm. Crystal swallowed the generous amount of semen that filled her mouth, then pushed herself to her knees.

"It's my turn now, people," Crystal announced. "Eva, why don't you help Larson get hard for me."

Eva reached for his flaccid penis and after two strokes, he stood straight up.

Crystal's eyes widened in amazement.

"Wow, you should teach me that trick."

Eva slid her mouth over his hard, hot flesh. He twitched and groaned in pleasure. Crystal stroked her own breasts as she watched, toying with her hard, sensitive nipples. She shifted one hand down to her pussy and glided her finger along her wet slit.

Eva pulled away from Larson, then shifted behind Crystal and wrapped her arms around her. Crystal sighed in delight as Eva's soft fingers caressed her breasts.

"Larson, why don't you kiss Crystal's pussy?" Eva suggested.

"Do you want me to, Eva?"

Eva smiled and nodded.

His gaze shifted to Crystal, his turquoise eyes filled with heat. "Do you want me to, Crystal?"

The soft skin of Eva's breasts pushed against Crystal's back as she reclined and spread her legs wider, longing for his tongue to invade her slick opening.

"You bet."

Crystal sighed as he dipped his face into her pussy, then arched at the delicious feel of his tongue stroking her clit. Eva's fingertips stroking over Crystal's nipples heightened the pleasure. Larson flicked his tongue rapidly over her clit as his fingers delved deep inside her. Heat built within her and then pleasure swelled through her. She arched again and moaned, then wailed in a long, heady climax.

Larson licked up Crystal's body and then his hot mouth captured one nipple, along with Eva's fingers, which were stroking it. When Eva tried to draw her hand away, he grasped her wrist. He sucked both Crystal's nipple and Eva's fingers at the same time. Crystal loved the erotic feel of Eva's fingers stroking her wet nipple inside Larson's hot mouth.

He claimed Crystal's mouth in a passionate kiss, his tongue pulsing deep into her. Then he released her and shifted his mouth to Eva's. He eased Eva back against the cushions, with Crystal settled in front of her. Then she felt his big cock press against her damp opening.

Oh, God, he was so big and hard. Crystal longed to feel him inside her. Slowly, his big shaft glided into her, filling her. Stretching her. Once he filled her completely, he drew back, his cockhead dragging along her vagina in an erotic caress. Then he thrust forward again, filling her even more deeply. Crystal cried out at the exquisite sensation.

He drew back and filled her again, and again, until he was plunging into her deep and hard. Eva's soft breasts crushed against Crystal's back with each forward thrust.

Larson's hands cupped Crystal's butt, then one shifted and Crystal felt it glide along her thigh. When Eva gasped, Crystal realized he must be stroking her clit. He continued to stimulate Eva as he drove into Crystal. Eva continued to tease Crystal's nipples with her fingertips as he pounded into her.

Crystal felt as if she would explode with pleasure. The sensations swelled and washed over her.

"Oh, God, I'm coming," Crystal cried, then wailed on a long, rising note.

Eva arched forward. "Oh, God, me too." Then she moaned as well.

Larson grunted and Crystal could feel his hot semen flooding her pussy.

They all slumped in a mass of satisfied flesh. Larson kissed Crystal sweetly, then his lips captured Eva's and her body trembled beneath Crystal.

It was so clear these two were deeply in love. Eva was fighting it, though. She needed a little encouragement to just let go and allow the man to make love to her like they both clearly wanted to. Desperately.

"That was great, you two. There's one more thing I'd like." She eased out from between them. Larson's heavy, damp cock fell on Eva's belly. "I want to watch the two of you."

Larson glanced at Eva but shook his head.

"I can't." He started to roll away from Eva.

Crystal pushed him back down. "Well, it will take a little work, but…"

"It's not that," Eva answered. "He's waiting for me to ask him." She slid her arms around him. "Larson, please. Make love to me."

His lips grazed Eva's neck and he nuzzled. He whispered something against her ear that Crystal couldn't hear.

Eva nodded. "Absolutely."

Immediately, he moved against Eva and she moaned as he positioned his big hard cock against her and slid inside. As Crystal watched, she immediately longed to feel that cock inside her again.

Actually, what she really wanted was to feel Terrien fill her like that. To feel Terrien's arms around her and see the loving look in his eyes as he gazed at her like Larson did Eva.

"Oh, yes, Larson. Make love to me."

He slid back, then forward again. Oh, God, Crystal wanted Terrien to make love to her.

"Do you like that, sweetheart?"

"Yes, oh, God, yes." Eva sucked in a breath.

The ache inside Crystal intensified. He sucked one of Eva's nipples deep into his mouth, then thrust forward.

"Deeper, Larson," Eva pleaded.

He propelled forward, filling her deeper.

"Faster and harder."

Oh, God, it was hot watching them.

He drove hard and fast. His solid length pounded into Eva. She wrapped her legs around him and moaned in pleasure. His fingers slid to her clit and he stroked. She cried out and her face contorted as an orgasm swept over her. Still he filled her again and again, then added a spiral motion. She screamed in abandon.

Crystal's pussy clenched as she longed for Terrien's big cock to drive into her. Her breasts swelled, aching for his touch.

Larson tensed, clearly filling Eva with his hot seed. Eva held him tightly against her.

Finally, they both collapsed against the pillows. His lips brushed hers in a tender, loving kiss.

Yes, those two were obviously in love.

"Thank you, darling Eva. That was incredible." Larson scooped her onto his lap and into a tight embrace. His lips found hers again and he kissed her deeply.

Then he turned to Crystal.

"Thank you, Crystal. You were fantastic," he said.

Crystal leaned forward and kissed him lightly. The man was definitely a gentleman.

"Thank you, sweetie." Crystal leaned toward Eva and kissed her too. "Hang on to this one, honey. You two are obviously meant to be together."

The words seemed to jar Eva from the spell she'd been under. Immediately, she closed up and Larson shifted away.

Crystal could see the pain in Larson's eyes and remembered the same look in Terrien's. Guilt washed through her.

She and Eva were two of a kind. Both fighting what was being thrust upon them. But in Eva's case, it was so clearly right for her to be with Larson. Anyone could see it. Crystal hoped the woman would figure that out in time.

It was different with Crystal, however. Crystal was not

meant to be tied down to one man. And she certainly couldn't allow herself to become dependent on one.

At least this tryst with Larson had taught her that Terrien wasn't the only man who could give her exciting and explosive orgasms. Larson's expertise had given her every bit as much pleasure as Terrien had. He'd brought her to the same stupendous, erotic heights.

At least, on a physical level.

Crystal watched as Larson tugged on his clothes. He left the quarters, promising to return with Terrien. Eva pulled on her robe while Crystal dressed and they went into the living room.

"What's wrong, sweetie?" Crystal sat in one of the armchairs in the living area. "Aren't you happy with your guy?"

"I could ask you the same thing." Eva settled in the chair across from her friend. "Why did you come here to be with Larson?"

Crystal shrugged. "You might have guessed by now, I'm not the type to be with just one guy. I'm not wired that way. I told Terrien that I wanted to sample more of the local cuisine, so to speak. I take it he chose Larson because they're friends, so he trusts him."

"And Terrien was okay with you being with someone else?"

Crystal shrugged again, hiding the guilt creeping through her. "I'm sure he figures this will prove to me that he's my one-and-only. That no other man can satisfy me the way he can."

"And?"

Crystal's heart ached as she realized it was true that

Larson could satisfy her physically, but there was a deeper need that he could not meet. A profound, intense yearning that only Terrien could satisfy.

Crystal took a deep breath. "I told you, I don't believe in soul-mates."

CHAPTER 12

Crystal sank back into the chair and gazed at Eva. "So tell me what's going on with you and Larson? Why all the rules?"

Eva hesitated, then sucked in a deep breath. "I... Ever since my divorce, I decided I'm in charge of my own pleasure."

Crystal could relate to that, but Eva clearly had bigger issues.

"In other words, you think Larson's going to hurt you."

Eva shifted uncomfortably.

"Your husband screwed around, right?" Crystal asked.

Eva nodded. "But even before that, when he made love to me, if you could call it that, he didn't care about me."

"He never gave you an orgasm?"

"No, he never even tried."

The bastard. Crystal knew so many women screwed up by selfish men. That's why Crystal had always taken control of her own pleasure. She would not be dependent on any man, for pleasure or anything else.

But it was so clear that Larson loved Eva and would do anything for her. She had nothing to worry about there.

Crystal leaned forward and took Eva's hand.

"Look, honey, that was him, and Larson is Larson. Obviously, Larson knows how to make love to a woman and it's obvious he really loves you. He'll always make sure you're happy."

Eva stared down at their linked hands.

"But how can I know?" Eva drew her hand away. "How can I take the chance?"

"Oh, God, honey. How can you not? How can you turn your back on a guy who's going to love you and bring you pleasure at every opportunity? Look how he held back when he obviously wanted to make love to you. He left himself totally at your mercy. How can you chance losing that?"

A few moments later, a buzz sounded and the door to the quarters slid open. The sight of Terrien in the doorway took Crystal's breath away. Everything she'd just said to Eva could be said of her and Terrien, too. She should be giving herself the same advice, but…

The thought of giving herself over to Terrien and the love that she now realized so clearly pulsed through her terrified her. A blind terror she could not even comprehend.

But the pain in Terrien's eyes haunted her.

Crystal clasped Eva's hand and squeezed, then stood up. Crystal avoided looking at Terrien as she crossed the room.

Silently, Crystal followed Terrien back to their quarters. As soon as the door closed behind them, Crystal headed into her bedroom, unable to face Terrien right now. The door closed behind her and she stripped off her dress and climbed into bed, then pulled the covers around her.

Oh, God, what would she do now?

Terrien had lain in bed all night, staring at Crystal's closed door, longing for her to be in his arms. Longing for her body pressed close to his. It tore at his heart that she'd gone to Larson yesterday, but then she'd closed herself away in her room. Closing herself off from him.

He pushed himself from his bed and showered, then trod into the kitchen. He made coffee and an omelet for Crystal, intending to knock on her door to invite her to join him for breakfast once it was done. As he placed it on the plate, however, he felt her presence behind him. He turned to see her watching him from the doorway, wearing a blue robe.

"Good morning," he said.

"Good morning." Her gaze slipped from his and she poured herself a cup of coffee.

"Did you sleep well?" he asked.

"No." She sipped her coffee. "I…thought about a lot of things."

His heart clenched. Was this a good or bad thing? From the way she avoided his gaze, he was afraid it was bad.

He handed her the plate.

"Thanks. It smells good." She took it and walked to the table, then sat down.

He served up his own omelet and sat across from her. They ate in silence. If she wanted to talk to him about her thoughts, it seemed she was waiting until after breakfast.

Definitely a bad thing.

Once she'd finished her meal, he gathered her plate and his and set them aside.

"So you thought about a lot of things last night. Would you like to share some of your thoughts?"

She gazed at him and nodded. Her forlorn expression told him this was a *very* bad thing.

"I…" She shook her head and sucked in a breath. "I don't want to hurt you, but…"

Heghat. His heart clenched. He was sure he didn't want to hear this.

"I can't do this," she continued. "I can't be your tannashay. I can't stay on this ship or your planet. I need to be free. I need to be independent."

"I don't intend to take away your independence."

She leaned forward. "Terrien, I can't do it. No matter what you intend, I will be on a different planet. I will have to depend on you. I don't know your culture. I don't know how to get a job or even what I'd do. I don't even know your language."

"Language is not an issue. You can learn it easily. We have technology to allow you to absorb a new language quickly and effortlessly. And as for a job, we don't have money. People are provided with all the basics and they can earn extra credit for luxuries if they wish. Since you are an artist, you will not only have total freedom to live and do whatever you want, you will have the means to live a very luxurious life."

"I'm not an artist. I paint as a hobby, but I can't make a living at it."

She'd been passionate about her art in high school, but she hadn't wanted to wind up like her mother, with no reliable way to support herself. Her sister had talked her into a career in marketing where, theoretically, she could make use of her artistic ability. Unfortunately, that hadn't happened, but she did earn a reasonable living.

"On *Sa'oul* you can. All art is held in high esteem, and since you are from another world, your work will be highly sought after. Believe me, Crystal, you will not be dependent on anyone."

Crystal drew in a deep breath and stared at her hands, her fingers interlaced.

It would be wonderful to spend her days painting rather than working in marketing at the hotel. But that was only one concern about being dependent on Terrien. The bigger concern—the one she could not get past—was her dependence on him sexually.

No, not sexually. It was because—her heart clenched painfully—she was in love with him and a woman in love made poor decisions. She'd seen that over and over again with her mother.

Crystal knew she could not let a man, or her emotions for a man, control her. She knew she had to walk away, no matter how much it would hurt.

She stood up, her hands clenched into fists.

"Terrien, the point is I don't believe in soul-mates and I don't intend to marry you, or live with you, or whatever it is you're expecting. I have a life on Earth and I'm happy with it. If you really care for me, you'll take me back to Earth."

"Crystal…"

She hazarded a glance at his face and wished she hadn't. The agony in his eyes tore through her.

"You can't mean it."

She nodded, tearing her gaze from his. "I do. If you really love me, let me go."

She turned around and strode back to her bedroom.

CHAPTER 13

Hours had passed since Crystal had made her request. Since then, she'd stayed in her room, expecting Terrien to come in and talk to her, to try to convince her to stay with him. But he didn't. Thank heavens.

"Crystal, may I come in?" Terrien's voice sounded through a speaker in the room.

She sighed and stood up, then crossed the room and opened the door.

He stood in the doorway, tall and rigid, facing her. "Do you understand if you go back to Earth, you will continue to feel our connection? Without me there to satisfy your yearning, it will be an agony that eats at you forever."

"You think a lot of yourself." Her light tone did not decrease the intensity of his dark green eyes.

"I'm not joking. It will never diminish," he insisted. "You know what I'm talking about. Even if you don't admit it, you felt it before I brought you here. It started slowly, then increased until it became almost unbearable. No man could satisfy the need."

Yes, she remembered. It had been totally frustrating, in

more ways than one, but she hadn't understood it then. But now she did and she would find a way to deal with it.

He stepped toward her and reached for her hand, but she stepped back. His mouth compressed into a straight line.

"Don't think because I will be back on *Sa'oul* that it will fade. Once the connection has been made, it is with you always."

She nodded. "So I'm always going to be hot for you. And I'll miss you. I'll learn to live with that."

He took her hand again but this time didn't let go when she tried to draw away. He stroked her hair from her face with such gentleness, tears prickled at her eyes.

"Why can't you just accept what there is between us? I love you."

Her heart ached and she blinked back tears, keeping them in check. "I'm sorry, Terrien, but...I just don't love you." It was the biggest lie of her life, but she had to say it. "Please, take me home."

He frowned, his green eyes glittering with emotion.

Finally, he released her hand and turned his back on her. "Pull your stuff together," he said in a hard voice as he walked through his bedroom toward the other door. "We leave in an hour."

Crystal glanced around at her familiar living room. She stood in her own apartment. On Earth.

The trip with Terrien aboard the small spacecraft had taken only a few hours. He said the smaller craft could travel at much higher speeds than the bulkier spaceship that had to carry so many people. She didn't understand the science behind it any more than she understood how a television worked, but she was thankful that she'd only had to spend a few hours with him rather than several days.

"Thank you. I appreciate you bringing me back."

Terrien simply nodded. He stood only feet from her, but she felt like he was miles away. Ever since she'd asked him to bring her back to Earth, he'd put up a barrier.

And, of course, that made sense, but the distance between them disturbed her.

Well, get used to it. Soon he'll be gone. For good.

"I have to leave," he said.

"Oh, do you have time for a coffee or something?" *Damn. How totally lame.*

"No, I need to pick up something, then return to the ship."

She nodded. "Okay, well… I guess this is good-bye."

The coolness in his eyes faltered and he stepped forward. "Crystal, are you sure you want to do this?"

Her heart ached and uncertainty swirled through her. But she had to be strong.

"I'm staying here, Terrien." She couldn't resist. She raised her hand and stroked his cheek, then along his rigid jaw. "I'm sorry."

Suddenly, she was in his arms, pressed tight to his solid body. Their lips met and his tongue sought hers. She succumbed to the sweet passion and melted against him, devouring his mouth as he devoured hers. Her body ached for him, her heart hammering in time with his.

Then he released her and stepped back.

He stared at her and the silence hung between them. She wanted to lurch forward and tell him she would go back with him. She would be his soul-mate and wife. They would live happily ever after together.

But real life wasn't like that.

Clearly, he saw the determination in her eyes. He sighed.

"Good-bye, Crystal."

He pulled a small controller from his pocket and pushed a button. Then he was gone.

Crystal glanced around her apartment, feeling a little out of place. Here she was, back at home after travelling in a spaceship far from Earth. She should be happy to be home, but it all seemed a little anticlimactic.

She walked into the kitchen and opened the fridge door, but all that was there were a few vodka coolers, some wilted lettuce, a half carton of milk she hadn't finished before she'd left on vacation, and some condiments. She grabbed a cooler and opened it, then poured it into a tall glass and added ice. She'd have to go out shopping and get some food, but that could wait until she was a little more settled in again.

She walked into the spare bedroom she had set up as her office and turned on the computer. Checking email seemed like a nice, ordinary task to pull her back into her regular life again. To help her feel settled.

Because right now she felt anything but settled. In fact, she felt very unsettled, her insides fluttering as if filled with butterflies. She was home. She should be happy.

But she wasn't. Memories of Terrien washed through her and her heart ached.

She opened her browser and glanced through the inbox at the long list of unread messages, then tried to lose herself in the mindless task of sorting through them. They were mostly newsletters she subscribed to, bill notifications, some work messages, et cetera.

Time slipped away, but thoughts of Terrien didn't.

She could feel the urgent longing she'd experienced before he'd come into her life, but now she recognized it for what it was. Back then, it had felt like lust. And it *had* been, in part. A need to join with him. To have him inside her body. Joined in an intimate way. In a *loving* way.

At first, since she'd never met him—didn't even know he

existed—it had hit her as a physical need for sex, but no man had satisfied that need because none of them had been the man she needed. The man she was meant to be with.

That man was Terrien.

A paralyzing ache surged through her.

Oh, God. What had she done?

This feeling inside her—this longing that gnawed at her insides—was a longing for him. And it would never diminish. It would never go away.

Oh, God, she was in love with Terrien. And she'd sent him away. Forever. He was gone from her life. And she couldn't do anything about it.

CHAPTER 14

Crystal stood and walked to the window, then stared out at the city below. There were people all around her. In the apartments surrounding hers. On the sidewalks below. In the restaurants, coffee shops, stores, and cars travelling along the streets. But she felt a profoundly deep loneliness. Because not one of these people could fill the need inside her.

Only Terrien could do that. Only he could fill her life with joy.

Damn it, why had she run away from what they had?

She needed to be independent. She needed control over her own life. But he'd never tried to control her. He'd even agreed to bring her home when she'd insisted, despite the fact that he knew that would steal away his happiness forever.

She clenched her fists. The stupid thing was, she had actually let her fear of being controlled control her. She had been more afraid of that than losing the man she loved. The only man who could make her happy.

And now she'd pay the price.

They'd both pay the price for her stupidity.

If only she had another chance. If only…

A knock sounded at her door and she dashed the tears from her eyes. Tears she hadn't even realized she'd shed. She walked down the hallway, thankful for something to take her mind off the pain, but when she crossed through the living room, she remembered Terrien standing in this room only a couple of hours ago and the tears welled again.

A knock sounded again. It must be the building manager, because anyone else would have had to buzz the intercom. She snatched a tissue from the box beside the couch and dried her eyes, then opened the door.

"Hello." There stood Terrien, his large muscular frame filling her doorway.

"Terrien?" The shock held her poised for only a split second, then she launched herself into his arms, joy surging through her.

He tightened them around her in a solid embrace as she consumed his mouth, gliding her tongue inside, following a primal need to join with him in some way. He thrust into her mouth and practically devoured her. He lifted her from the ground and carried her inside, kicking the door closed behind them.

As her feet touched the ground again, she released his lips and stared into his glittering green eyes. Then he smiled, lighting up his entire face, and joy washed through her.

"Miss me?" he asked.

Damn, he looked so smug. He knew this would happen!

In answer, she stripped off her top and pulled down the cups of her bra, revealing her hard, aroused nipples. Then she stroked over the growing bulge in his pants.

"As much as you missed me." She unzipped him, then reached inside and found his hot, hard cock.

He groaned as she stroked him.

"Oh, God, Crystal." He backed her against the wall, his eyes smoldering with need.

He unfastened her jeans and she pushed them down, her panties along with them. She took his hand and placed it over her pussy, then guided his finger along her slick opening.

"I want you, Terrien." She grasped his cock and placed the tip against her slit. He groaned, then pushed forward, filling her with his incredibly thick cock. She gasped at the astonishing pleasure it gave her. Not just physical, but deep in her soul. She leaned forward and nibbled his ear. As he drew back and glided into her again, she murmured, "I love you, Terrien."

He stopped, fully impaled inside her, with her crushed against the wall, and he stared at her. The profound glow of love in his eyes sent her heart into a spin.

Then he smiled. "I love you too, Crystal."

His lips met hers and passion consumed them both. He drew back and thrust forward again. Then again. Without warning, a wave of absolute joy washed over her, then catapulted to full-fledged ecstasy. She moaned as he drove into her, sending her to heights she'd never even dreamed of. As bliss exploded through her, she clung to him, knowing she would never let go of this man ever again. She was his. And he was hers. They belonged together.

As she gasped for breath, he nuzzled her neck.

"Does this mean you've changed your mind?" Terrien murmured against her skin.

"No, of course not."

His head jerked up so fast she worried he'd have whiplash. She had to stop herself from laughing out loud.

"I still love you," she said, a devilish smile on her face.

He still seemed uncertain and now she felt cruel. She

grabbed his collar and pulled him toward her for another kiss.

"I want to go home."

"You are home, Crystal."

She shook her head. "No." She glanced around. "This is just an apartment." She locked gazes with him. "Home is where you are."

EPILOGUE

Crystal gathered a few things from her room and put them in a bag, then grabbed her laptop. The latter mostly because it had her personal photos on it. Terrien told her they would be able to convert the data she wanted into a form she could use on his world's version of computers.

She also gathered the paintings she'd done along with her paint supplies. Terrien took the portfolio and paint case and set them by her bag in the living room.

"Are you ready?" he asked.

She nodded. He took her hand and pressed the button on the little remote device he carried. Seconds later, they appeared in the small ship that had brought them from the larger spacecraft back to Earth.

A plastic case with circular holes sat on the floor near one of the passenger seats. A distinctive sound—actually more like a complaint—emanated from the cage.

"Is that a cat?" Crystal asked as she circled the box. On the other side, she saw a barred door. A small cat peered out at her and mewed.

She glanced at Terrien. "Did you get me a cat?"

"No, that is Aria's cat, Rex. After you told me how people get attached to cats and other pets, we double-checked the other Earth women's files and found that Aria had a cat. The captain sent me to retrieve him."

"So that's what you did after you dropped me here? Went to get Aria's cat?"

"Yes."

"And you decided to check on me again before you left?"

"I couldn't leave without trying one more time to convince you to come back with me."

She leaned down and smiled at the little cat. "Hey, there, fella. You're now officially my new best friend."

Terrien laughed as he opened the cage and let the cat out. It prowled around the small spaceship, exploring everything with great interest. Terrien sat in the pilot's chair and Crystal sat in the chair beside him. As Terrien put the ship in motion, the cat leaped onto Crystal's lap. She stroked its little head, then along its sleek, furry body. It purred loudly.

Crystal laughed, loving the soothing sound and the warm fuzzy feeling it gave her. Maybe having a cat wouldn't be such a bad idea. She glanced at Terrien, who piloted the ship with a wide smile on his face.

After all, the choice to welcome a man into her life had been a satisfying one.

Her heart pounded as she realized she'd finally accepted that Terrien was her soul-mate. The man she would spend the rest of her life with. She almost felt faint, but not from trepidation, as she'd feared after making this irrevocable decision. Instead, joy swelled through her.

Because she knew, to the core of her being, that she had made the right choice. Because she had chosen love.

~

AFTERWORD

*I hope you enjoyed **Rebel Mate**.*

If you did, please post a review at your favorite online store because that's the best way to help me write more stories like this.

If not, please email me at <u>Opal@OpalCarew.com</u> because I love to hear from my wonderful readers.

FREE EBOOKS

Would you like more hot, sexy stories?
Join the Opal Carew Reader Group
to receive free erotic reads!

Just go to
OpalCarew.com/ReaderGroup

Patreon.com/OpalCarew

EXCERPTS

Rebel Mate is the third story to be released of the five-story **Abducted** series. Keep an eye open for **Illicit Mate** which will be released soon! (These stories can be read in any order.)

In **Rebel Mate,** Crystal was up for anything. For more stories about women who are ready for anything, check out **Hot Ride**, the first of Opal's **Ready to Ride** series of extremely hot biker romances.

If you'd like to see more of Opal's sci-fi romance, you'll love **Virtual Love** by Amber Carew (Opal's slightly milder pseudonym) about a woman who finds her virtual reality fantasies invaded by a sexy stranger.

Finally, if you want something a lot hotter, check out **Jenna's Punishment** by Ruby Carew (Opal's erotica pseudonym) about a woman who finds out that some secrets are worth pursuing, especially when discovering them means you might be punished!

All of the above stories can be found at **OpalCarew.com**
Here is an excerpt for **Hot Ride**…

HOT RIDE

OPAL CAREW

Hot, hard, fast, and handles like a dream!
Oh yeah, and the bike's not bad either.

Hayley is looking for more excitement in her life, but doesn't know how to find it.

Excitement finds Rip, a biker who's seen more than his share of trouble.

When trouble finds Rip yet again and a bar brawl starts, both he and Hayley are thrown to the curb.

Hayley knows this is her chance to find the excitement she so craves, but Rip doesn't want to be some good girl's bad-boy experience, so he turns down her advances, leaving her feeling rejected.

But life is never that simple for Rip, and he soon finds himself in her bed and wanting more. When his three biker friends show up, Hayley's love of numbers turns into an erotic adventure none of them will ever forget.

But is there a chance for more than that between Hayley and Rip? Find out by taking a Hot Ride you'll never forget.

Excerpt

The young woman—Hayley—gazed at Rip, her eyes widened. Well, fuck, of course she'd be nervous about walking down a dark alley with the likes of him. If she were his sister, he wouldn't want her taking a chance like that.

He took her hand and raised it to his mouth. The feel of her soft skin as he brushed his lips against it made him long to feel more of her. His groin tightened at the thought of kissing her, then exploring her round, beautiful breasts. The creamy swell of them exposed by her deep neckline had been teasing him all evening.

"I promise. I'll get you to your hotel, safe and sound."

She stared into his eyes, mesmerized, then she nodded.

He smiled and took her hand, then led her into the alley. A cat darted in front of them, startling her. She drew close to him, clutching his arm. The feel of her warm, soft body pressed to his side sent his hormones to alert status, but he ignored that and slipped his arm around her protectively, drawing her close. It didn't help that he kept remembering when her gaze had dropped to his crotch with obvious interest after he'd told her about his name. He was glad she didn't know that he actually got the name because his fellow bikers had caught him reading Ripley's Believe It or Not one day.

She took another step, but then stopped. "There's another problem."

"What's that?"

"Well, I'm basically barefoot, and I have no idea what might be on the ground ahead."

"Right. I'm pretty sure I saw broken glass near where I parked the bike."

"I could hobble along with my broken—Oh!"

He scooped her up into his arms and she slid her hands around his shoulders.

Oh, God, Hayley felt so tiny and light in this big man's arms. She could stay here all day, lulled in his embrace. As he walked, the gentle rocking of his body soothed her.

"We're here."

Her eyelids popped open. Had she really dozed off? The combination of white wine spritzers, a long flight in, and staying up way too late last night finishing up work, since she was taking an extra long weekend, was knocking her on her butt.

She glanced toward a big, powerful looking motorcycle parked close to the brick wall. It was black and intimidating, adorned with a blazing red and orange flame. It had shiny chrome wheels and a big, black leather seat.

"It's nice," she said as he carried her toward it.

"Nice?" He chuckled and set her on her feet beside it. "Maybe big. Dangerous. Powerful." He grinned. "But nice?"

Oh, God, he was big and dangerous and powerful. Everything she dreamed of when she thought about her wildest fantasies coming true. And here he was, smiling down at her. She already missed his strong arms around her.

She gazed into his midnight blue eyes. "I like big, dangerous and powerful." She stepped closer and flattened her hand on his hard, muscular chest. The feel of rock-solid, sculpted muscles under the thin fabric of his T-shirt set her heart thumping. "Like you."

She dropped her shoes and purse, and slid her hands over his shoulders then stroked his raspy cheek. His eyes simmered with heat as she tipped up her face, then drew him toward her. His mouth brushed hers lightly, and she flicked her tongue against his lips and slid timidly inside. He growled and deepened the kiss, wrapping his arms around her and pulling her tighter to his hard body, then gliding his tongue deep into her mouth.

She melted against him, heat simmering through her. But then he drew back.

"This isn't a good idea."

She blinked at his words. He was rejecting her?

"Don't you find me attractive?"

"It's not that."

Feeling bolder than she ever had, and determined not to let this opportunity slip away, she grasped his hand and drew it to her chest, then placed it over her aching breast. Her nipple hardened, pushing into his palm.

His dark eyes glowed like a blazing fire, glittering with sparks.

In a sudden movement, she felt herself pushed back against the building. Her breath caught as his big, solid body crushed her tight to the cold brick wall.

Oh, God, had she made a mistake? He was so big and intimidating, and right now, he looked determined and… almost feral. He pivoted his hips forward and she could feel a hard bulge against her stomach, proof that he was aroused by her. Anxiety spiked through her, and a little fear, but right alongside those feelings was a wild surge of excitement.

He grabbed her wrists and pushed them over her head, then held them tight, his striking midnight eyes locked on hers. She could feel the erratic pounding of her blood pumping through her veins.

She had never felt so alive.

God, she wanted him to take her. Right here. Right now.

~

#1: The Office Slave

(aka Red Hot Fantasies #3)

#2: The Boss

#3: On Her Knees

#4: Her New Master

#5: Please, Master

#6: Yes, Sir

#7: On His Knees

Red Hot Fantasies series

#1: The Male Stripper

#2: The Stranger

#3: The Office Slave

#4: The Captive

(prequel to Mastered by her Captor)

#5: The Bridal Affair

Ready To Ride biker series

Hot Ride

Wild Ride

Riding Steele

Hard Ride

Three series

#1: Three

#2: Three Men and a Bride

#3: Three Secrets

Futuristic erotic romance novellas

Slaves of Love

Abducted series

(formerly Celestial Soul-Mates series)

Forbidden Mate

Unwilling Mate

Rebel Mate

Illicit Mate

Captive Mate

Fantasy erotic romance

Crystal Genie

Collections and Anthologies

Submitting to His Rules

Mastered by the Boss

Mastered by the CEO

Surrendering to His Rules

Mastered by her Captor

Mastered by the Sheikh

Owned by the Sheikh

Mastered by the Sheikh

Debt of Honor

Slaves of Love

Total Surrender

Played by the Master

The Office Slave

Three

Dirty Talk, Books 1 & 2

Dirty Talk, Books 3 & 4

Dirty Talk, The Complete Series

The Office Slave Series, Book 1 & 2

The Office Slave Series, Book 3 & 4

The Office Slave Series, Book 5 & 6

The Office Slave Series, Book 7 & Bonus

Red Hot Fantasies, Volume 1 (Books 1-3)

Red Hot Fantasies, Volume 2 (Books 4-5)

Ready to Ride, Book 1 & 2

Three Happy Endings (Books 1-3)

Turn Up The Heat (anthology)

Slaves of Love

Northern Heat (anthology)

Three

∼

Contemporary erotic romance novels

Stroke of Luck

X Marks the Spot

Heat

A Fare To Remember

Nailed

My Best Friend's Stepfather

Stepbrother, Mine

Hard Ride

Riding Steele

His To Claim

His To Possess

His To Command

Illicit

Insatiable

Secret Weapon

Total Abandon

Pleasure Bound

Bliss

Forbidden Heat

Secret Ties

Six

Blush

Swing

Twin Fantasies

Contemporary erotic romance (ebook only)

Meat

Big Package

Drilled

ALSO BY RUBY CAREW

Contemporary erotic short story series

Stacy and Her Dad's Best Friend series

Jenna's Best Friend's Father series

Tempting the Boss series

All He Wants series

Collections and Anthologies

Stacy and Her Dad's Best Friend - Collection 2

Jenna's Best Friend's Father - Collection 1

Tempting the Boss - Collection 1
Tempting the Boss - Collection 2

All He Wants – Christmas Collection

ALSO BY AMBER CAREW

Romance Novels

Contemporary

In Too Deep

The Cinderella Obsession

Virgin Wanted

Fantasy

Christmas Angel

I Dream of Genie

Spellbound

Futuristic

Virtual Love

ABOUT THE AUTHOR

Opal Carew is a *New York Times* and *USA Today* bestselling author of erotic romance. Her books have won several awards, including the National Readers' Choice Award (twice), the Golden Leaf Award (twice), the Golden Quill (4 times), CRA Award of Excellence, and Silken Sands.

Opal writes about passion, love, and taking risks. Her heroines follow their hearts and push past the fear that stops them from realizing their dreams... to the excitement and love of happily-ever-after.

Opal loves nail polish, cats, crystals, dragons, feathers, pink hair, the occult, Manga artwork, Zentangle, and all that glitters. She grew up in Toronto, and now lives in Ottawa with her husband, huge nail polish collection, and five cats.

One of her sons just finished his second Masters degree in Geopolitics (first at Sussex University in the UK and second at Carleton University in Ottawa.) The other son is doing his Masters at the University of Toronto. Yes, mom is proud!

Social Media Links

Reader Group: OpalCarew.com/ReaderGroup
Patreon: OpalCarew
Website: OpalCarew.com
Facebook: OpalCarewRomanceAuthor

Twitter: @OpalCarew
Pinterest: opalcarew
Goodreads: bit.ly/OC_Goodreads
Contact Opal: bit.ly/contactopal